The Kat & Denney Archives:
Bourbon & Benjamins

Kathy Steele and Linda George

for my fellow FCRWC member

Linda George

The Kat & Denney Archives: Bourbon & Benjamins
Kathy Steele and Linda George

Orange Horse Press
3735 Palomar Centre Dr.
Ste. 150 (#35)
Lexington KY 40513
https://www.katanddenneyarchives.com/

Cover Design: **www.RickFeeney.com**

Dedication

This book is dedicated to our family, who has had an ongoing interest in finishing this book.

Bourbon & Benjamins

Acknowledgments

We want to thank Lisa Haneberg with the Carnegie Center for Literacy and Learning, Susan Edwards with Reedsy for their encouragement and professional help, and Rick Feeney of Richardson Publishing for his invaluable publishing advice, keeping it simple for us and his thorough third overview.

We want to thank our Beta Readers for their early support and reviews:
Janet Barnhouse
H. "Charlie" Brown
Ken Crawford
Michelle Fillipelli
Adrianne Gilley
Alan Jones
Rob Miller
Bob Perry
Emma Phillips
Marie Ventarelli
Mary Alice White

With much appreciation to Adrianne and Matt Gilley for our web design.

Bourbon & Benjamins

Contents

Bourbon & Benjamins

Prologue

Instead of freshly rinsed air, a dense blanket of steam rose from the sidewalk. Kat stepped out on the porch of her Greek Revival house in the historic garden district of New Orleans and surveyed the street. A few puddles remained where a part of the sidewalk settled below the slab next to it, but nothing she couldn't step over. The trees shading the walk were still dripping from the just-ended spring shower. Kat allowed that this might be refreshing.

She locked the solid wooden door behind her and slid a five-dollar bill inside her shoe in case her jog took her by Starbucks. She hung the door key on a chain around her neck and clipped her phone on the waistband of her white jogging shorts. She tucked her hair under her favorite NASA ball cap.

At the curb, she looked both ways and decided to stay on the sidewalk. It was steeper than the walkway through the park, which made it less wet. She could jog past some of the aged and lovely landscaping in the District and pick up a few ideas.

Her sister, Denney, was in New York City, and she wondered how steamy it must be there with all the tall buildings and concrete.

***

In New York City, Denney, Kat's sister, was in a high-rise building, pacing in her psychiatrist's office.

"I'm telling you, my throat constricted, and my shoulders were so tightly clenched I could've been a floor joist." Denney paused and then went on. "So, I slipped out of the den, into the kitchen, and took several deep breaths—like you told me to do. Honestly, I felt homicidal rage. The tension eased only long enough for me to pour some three-day-old wine into an iced tea glass and call you."

Denney caught herself. She was so stressed that only now did she realize how pedestrian her options had become. There wasn't even any bourbon in the house. She watched as her psychologist first looked at her and then leafed through several pages of handwritten notes. His demeanor was thoughtful but relaxed as he sat across from her with uncrossed legs, her file on his lap. He seemed at ease even in his suit and tie. Behind him was a wall full of diplomas and certificates, although he never acted like he was more intelligent than anyone else. Then he looked up, intently focusing on Denney. "It seems as if your interactions are always the same. How do you feel about that?"

"I did it again! Same guy, different suit! I used to think I could survive this shit sandwich by just eating the crust. Now, I'm hungry, and I need more sandwich without the shit!"

Denney's psychologist leaned forward. "Where would you like to see yourself in six months or a year?"

* * *

Kat was about halfway through her jog. Her ball cap felt like a sauna. Her new wicking shorts and shirt were falling short of the advertised promise. She was thinking of her sister Denney when her cell rang. She stepped under the shade of a magnolia tree to take the call. Her palms were moist, and her finger slid across the screen twice as she tried to press the "connect" icon. She was out of breath and said only, "Yes."

"It's time," Denney said. "Soon, I'll be single again. Now we can pitch in together and get a place, just as we used to talk about!"

"Shut uuppp! Really?"

"Really."

Chapter 1

Where's the Money?

Two years had passed. Denney stayed in New York City until her divorce was final, then joined Kat. She was with Kat in their Phillip Street house in New Orleans when they heard from Vicar Dick that their father, known to most people as the Colonel, would sell his house in Louisville, Kentucky. She and Kat wasted no time in getting to Louisville. After some negotiation, they worked out a deal to buy it contract-for-deed and pay the Colonel in installments. It made the house easy for them to get into, but the Colonel maintained the lion's share of occupancy rights and an income from the contract installments. Not one to sign over all his interest in anything to anyone, he relied on the law to settle matters.

Kat and Denney closed their home in New Orleans to return to their Louisville home to start some much-needed renovation while the Colonel was off to parts unknown.

Denney spent most of the day opening the interior of the house. Kat tidied up the grounds and took the covers off the wicker porch furniture and prepared the porch for their early evening Manhattans.

Kat was eager to sit and enjoy the view. The weather had turned cool, and she looked forward to relaxing in the fresh air. She called to Denney to join her on the front, wraparound porch of their old Victorian home.

Denney made it to the porch carrying a tray of Manhattans. She had prepared them neat because of the cooler weather that evening.

The now "fifty-something" sisters, snuggled in oversized sweaters, were enjoying a sixty-degree early evening while sipping their Manhattans. Kat wore colorful sweaters, largely earth tones but usually with a bright pop of color and solid leggings. Denney wore monotone tunic-length cowl-neck sweaters with matching leggings or skinny jeans.

"Tomorrow is hump day," said Kat. She knew Denney always looked forward to the weekend. Denney was retired now, and Wednesday became the unofficial beginning of the weekend. Kat had not worked a full-time job in years because she gambled a lot and won most of the time.

Once comfortable on the porch, Kat pored over the stack of unpaid bills she'd brought out with her. She sat across from her sister, who was reading the evening paper. "Geez, paying these bills—why, it's absurd *and* unlikely that we can pay all of them," Kat moaned. "Look at this one, Denney. Two hundred dollars to *Petz*. What's this for?"

Denney glanced over the top of her cherry-red reading glasses. "The fur babies needed new beds—I told you."

Kat moved on. "Well, what about this one from the Shoe Emporium for $400.00?"

Denney felt this was becoming a one-sided inquisition and reached over and grabbed a couple of the unopened bills. "Oh, okay, what about this one." She waved the opened invoice in front of Kat. "It appears that you renewed your gym membership and added the VIP level for an additional $1,200. What's that about?"

Kat pursed her lips. "That's for access to the smoothie bar. Arturo makes the creamiest spinach and fruit-of-the-day concoctions. Add a little rum and it could rival Merriweather's coffee." Merriweather, a close friend of Kat and Denny's, was widely recognized among their small community for her potent rum and coffee.

"Let's stop talking about what we owe. We have plenty of money for the near future. Yes, we'll need to start thinking about what the Colonel may have left us. He's been dead for six months. That is certainly important, and once we find our inheritance, we'll be set until the end," Denny replied flatly.

"Our inheritance, you say?" Kat had become frustrated and starting pacing. "We have no paperwork that justifies that remark. What makes you think there is something out there for us from our Father?"

"Because the Vicar said he knew Father had holdings but would not make a will," said Denney. "We are his only heirs, so naturally, whatever he had would come to us. Knowing our father, it would be substantial. We just need to be patient and find it."

"But at his funeral, months ago, neither Vicar Dick nor anyone else approached us as to what that might be. No one has done so to this day. So, what are we depending on?" questioned Kat.

"It looks like we need to sit down with Vicar Dick and see what he knows at some point, as they were also friends," responded Denney. She laid the other invoice aside. "Okay, for the sake of argument, even if there is no inheritance, which I don't believe, if we need to cut back, it can't just be me."

"Yeah, I guess," Kat responded weakly as she also laid the remaining bills aside. She observed Denney exhaling a considerable amount of air as she moved on to the society section of the paper, signaling an end to the discussion.

Just then, a breeze wafted across the porch, causing the unpaid bills to flutter to the floor where Rusty, Kat's parti-color cocker spaniel, began to tear them apart and lovingly eat them.

Not bothering to correct Rusty, Kat picked up a section of the newspaper containing her horoscope. Reading it appealed to the gambler inside her. She liked playing the odds. Would the horoscope come true?

The other dogs, Jules, the mixed breed, and Gus, the schnauzer, rested contentedly, dozing off and on at the sisters' feet. Rusty continued his manic preoccupation.

Kat propped her feet up on another wicker chair while Denney still lounged across from her. Between them, a glass-topped wicker table held their drinks and a snack.

Denney took a sip of her Manhattan, followed by a bite of her watercress sandwich, and thought about how she hated the saying "hump day." Tomorrow would be Wednesday again. She remembered saying "hump day" to a person who had not been in this country long and was unfamiliar with the idiom. And yet, the woman was familiar enough with the street connotation to look embarrassed and piqued at the thought of a day to hump.

Feeling uncomfortable with the woman's response, Denney had leaped into an apologetic explanation, trying to explain that the "hump" was the middle of the week and likened it to the hump on a camel's back and how that was a metaphor for the downward slide to the weekend.

The woman had continued to stare at Denney blankly and gave her a weak smile as she turned and left. Denney was caught between wishing people would try harder to learn the language or at least act like it until they could Google it.

Why should she fall all over herself to justify a conversation that was just an effort at being friendly? Recalling this situation, she often dropped the f-bomb in her thoughts, but never, or at least very, very rarely aloud. She just couldn't imagine a scenario where it might be appropriate to utter it aloud.

Kat stood up and moved to sit on the stoop. The only thing worse than swimming so hard and going under was treading water until exhaustion set in. Trying to figure out their father and his motives was exhausting. Even as an adult, she still resented the fact that he had little regard for her and her sister. He ignored them. Had it not been for their mother, they would not have felt any love from a parental figure at all.

Sitting there, she felt a heaviness emanate from the house. The Colonel had lived in the house as a boy and well into adulthood when he was dubbed the Colonel. He received the title of Kentucky Colonel from the Governor after winning a bet on the golf course. He was in his early twenties, and the unlikely moniker not only stuck but began to define him.

The residence had been in the family since the late 1800s when it was built. The men in the family were known to have frequented the Pink Palace in those early days. This "Palace" was a grand house on the corner of St. James and Belgravia Court and was then a stately Gentleman's Club. All the influential patrons hobnobbed there, and many a lucrative deal started with a gentleman's handshake and was punctuated with an expensive cigar from Havana.

By virtue of living in one of the residences and one of the earliest mansions in the Southern Extension, Kat and Denney were Old Louisville denizens. Indeed, the Colonel's name was engraved on a brass plaque that once hung in the Pink Palace. The plaque now rested peacefully in the glass curio in their home.

Kat marveled at the St. James Fountain, a masterpiece that sat in the middle of the green space separating the East and West sides of St. James Court, and she often discussed with Denney how it was their favorite landmark.

Over the years, they had donated to its upkeep and many other local civic causes. Watching crystal clear water spilling from one level of the fountain provided a sense of timelessness and that all was right with the world, at least most of the time.

Chapter 2

Flasks of Manhattans

Kat, sitting in the kitchen, took a healthy swallow of her coffee and moodily addressed Denney. "Speaking of passing the time, we've forgotten about that bucket to fill for the church."

The bucket had become a significant source of irritation since it had initially been their idea. Kat and Denney would fill the buckets with trinkets and pass them out during the St. Patrick's Day parade. They felt the whole idea had been hijacked by Hulda Meisterman when she changed the intent.

"We need odds and ends for the outreach to those deadbeat guys," said Kat.

Denney eyed the five-gallon, green bucket sitting on the side table. "How did our fun participation in a parade turn into sponsoring deadbeat dads?" Denney responded with considerable animus.

"Well, it's not my fault." Kat was not one to mince words. "It was Hulda, that bossy woman, at church." She buried her feet under Rusty's warm body, his stomach gurgling softly.

Denney was exasperated. "Well, okay, did you talk with Hulda about this penchant she has for her new pet project? Buckets of Love. U*gh*! We participated in the parade for four years when she unilaterally took over the idea and turned it into her charity event." She continued to down her coffee and wanted to ignore the whole subject as her body tensed and tightened in her chair. She glanced over and noticed that Gus and Rusty raised their heads as if in expectation. They moved closer to her chair. She surmised what was about to happen. The dogs sat at attention, eyeing her bagel—just waiting for a crumb to fall.

Kat's voice took on a peevish tone as she frowned at Denney's preoccupation with picking at her napkin. "Denney, your denial is nothing short of palpable—not lost on me, I want you to know! I don't want to mess with the bucket either."

Kat finished her coffee and went upstairs to shower and get ready for the day.

Denney fixed another cup of coffee and remained in the kitchen. The soft morning light from outside the house cast a warm glow into the room. She thought about how she had developed renovation plans. Once the Colonel entered into the contract to sell them the house, he never returned to Louisville.

She knew what Kat liked also. She felt this was an excellent opportunity to put her stamp on it. The leaded-glass windows were still in fine shape. The woodwork was scuffed but responded to some TLC. However, the plaster walls needed a lot of work. The kitchen was taken down to the original brick walls. Studs were added, the walls were insulated, and drywall was hung on all but one wall, where the interior brick was exposed. Some of the original cabinets were reclaimed, and new cabinets were special-ordered to preserve the original feel of the home while adding modern amenities like soft-close drawers and pull-out shelving.

The baths were entirely remodeled under her critical eye. Only baths that guests used were renovated with touches meant to preserve the past.

Each sister had a large bedroom, and some of the available space was converted to a more modern master bath for each. Denney had considered putting pedestal sinks and claw-foot tubs in their baths, but on reconsideration, decided that they did not want to have to use steps to enter the tub or have to call one another, or worse, EMS, to get themselves out of the tubs. They both preferred large walk-in showers with benches.

Original closet space was minimal. Even though Kat tried to convince everyone that she wasn't fussy about her clothing, Denney knew she needed a large closet for her hundred pairs of shoes and equally large number of expensive handbags and sweaters.

Denney leaned toward a Caribbean Colonial style she had somehow picked up from the Colonel and incorporated this into the house aesthetic.

It was now mid-morning as she paused and sat motionless, contemplating the renovations she had overseen and the cost of it all. The woodwork had been meticulously refinished before the heat of summer could cause the lacquered finish to dry badly and blister. She concluded that the real plaster renovation was the capstone of her marvelous design.

The plaster repair was a nightmare but looked fabulous now. The new windows allowed in quite a bit of light. The thought of losing this personal sanctuary, as it had become, worried and saddened her, and Denney knew it upset Kat as well.

She had finished her coffee and bagel. The dogs hung their heads as if dismayed to be left with nothing to lap up. She patted their heads and muttered something about a fat farm for dogs. She gathered up the breakfast dishes, grabbed her tablet from the mahogany open secretary desk to check her email, and said to Gus, "Are you coming, baby?"

Both Rusty and Gus followed her up the stairs, Rusty turning to go to Kat's room and Gus following Denney. Jules was already at the top of the stairs, waiting.

Chapter 3

Brass Plated Good Deed

Hump day had arrived. Kat, the early riser, went to the front porch and grabbed the imposing, big and empty donation bucket. She returned to the kitchen and placed it in the middle of the table. Kat loved lattes and loved making them—especially the foam. She had her foam maker beside the French press. As she was making her latte, Denny slowly walked downstairs.

Denney entered the kitchen and yawned. "Ahh, the aroma of the fresh coffee!" The freshly ground beans sent a wave of energy through her nostrils, right to the action center of her brain. She could feel her very pleasure center break out in song.

Not having had her pep pill yet, she hoped fresh coffee would help reduce the fog and get her on track. Then she saw the bucket on the table. "Kat, you have *the* most perverse sense of timing. Why do we have to do this again? Can't someone else do this damn bucket for once?"

Kat leaned against the counter and looked at her. She then shifted her gaze to the bucket. "Well, it's now or never. I thought we could roll the dice or something," she said with forbearance.

Denney moaned.

Kat's eyes narrowed. "You know you could do something other than revising that script for the community theater production next month," she huffed. "Have you had your psychoactive substance yet?"

"You mean my green tea extract? I don't take bath salts, you know," she hissed. "Why don't *you* just do it?" Denney said dismissively. "You're already dressed, and I'm still in my pajamas." She liked to stress the obvious.

Kat was in her skinny jeans, Salty Dog long-sleeve tee-shirt, and flip-flops. Denney was still in her silk pajamas, and while fabulous, she thought, she wasn't ready to go anywhere.

Kat, already standing, admitted that she hated the bucket, too, but didn't feel like sharing the thought. After all, the bucket had initially been the sisters' idea for the St. Patrick's Day parade. They filled it with beads and green candies for four years and tossed them to the onlookers lining the route. They'd take the youth group from church and walk alongside the church float, tossing trinkets. She and Denney had their flasks of Manhattans in their fanny packs and at the ready.

The parade had stretched to three miles starting with the third season. Kat, fearing their flasks would not last three slow miles, stationed Ashleigh Daggit, whom they referred to as friend at roughly the one-and-a-half-mile point, and he handed them opaque water bottles filled with freshly made Manhattans. She felt Ashleigh had become a normal part of their lives, even if by default.

By the fourth season, the church informed Kat that it no longer wished to enter a float. But the youth had lobbied Vicar Dick because they still liked being in the parade with the sisters leading them even if they didn't have a float. The church, bowing to pressure from the youth, allowed the sisters to enter the parade as walkers. Both she and Denney reluctantly agreed.

Even though they did not have a church float in the parade, no one seemed to mind or question the sisters' presence.

In Kat's search to find an entrant to walk alongside, she found Krissy and her Yoga Goats. Krissy, dressed in a green sequined yoga top and pants, and driving a new gold Chevy Silverado, had her four barely visible goats riding in the truck bed. Now and then, one of them would bleat and raise its head enough to give the onlookers a better glimpse of pink nose.

Krissy would stop the truck long enough to allow Denney and Kat to ride in the bed with her goats if Denney signaled they were tired. It was easy to drink continuously while tossing a few hundred trinkets over their shoulders from that vantage point. Ashleigh, as was the tradition, was stationed along the way with fresh Manhattans.

Green and gold plastic bead necklaces, small green bow ties, and green wrapped mint candies flew into the crowd. Undoubtedly, Denney thought, their unchecked abandonment, while throwing trinkets and decorating the goats with strings of beads, substantially improved

Krissy's marketing.

It was during the fourth and last parade, Kat turned to Denney and remarked, "Denney, look!"

Denney stopped throwing trinkets and looked around. "What am I supposed to see?"

"Come closer. Look where I'm pointing." At that, the crowd started to cheer as if they had been selected for some great recognition. Kat tossed three handfuls of trinkets to them. Then, looking at Denney, Kat said, "See that guy in the blue shirt at the back of the sidewalk?"

Denney squinted. "You mean walking there by the shoe repair?"

"Yes. Is that Ashleigh?"

Denney paused. "How could it be? He met us four blocks ago and could never have walked this far by now. Wasn't he wearing a plaid shirt?"

Kat's gaze followed the fellow as long as possible before he was lost in the crowd. "Well, it sure looked like him. Uncanny!"

Denney grabbed some more beads and turned to continue tossing them. "Mother always said we all have a doppelganger."

The parade route was about to end, so Kat took the remaining trinkets and tossed them to the dwindling crowd as Denney looked once again at the sidewalk.

After the fourth year, the Parish Life Committee again decided to change up the St. Patrick's Day celebration. The parade and trinkets had been frivolous and fun, but now the event took on the overtones of somber and serious—as what was once just an amusing diversion morphed into the "brass-plated" good deed. Kat recalled with some feeling of betrayal the meeting when Hulda Meisterman, the Parish Life Committee chair, came up with the idea at a church vestry meeting that different groups within the church would fill buckets with handy items on a selected theme. One year it was unwed mothers. The buckets held a lot of pacifiers, baby wipes, and what have you. These were Hulda's "Buckets of Love." Another year they focused on retirement homes. Denney conceded they enjoyed the retirement home bucket the most and purchased loads of airplane-sized bottles of liquor. Kat picked up decks of large print playing cards. Shopping was invigorating that year.

This was the third year after their involvement with the parade. Kat realized it was her year to lead the committee's effort. She assumed that Denney would be on board, but Denney balked at this assumption because she had grown to despise the whole idea.

This year the buckets were for men who just never could find a job that suited them to support their family. Therefore, they were experiencing all the problems associated with lifelong unemployment, jail time, non-support, and who knew what else.

Kat had no use for people who thought they were too good, too smart, or over-qualified to work at a J-O-B. She struggled with filling this bucket because what in the world could she put in it? As a last-ditch effort, Kat picked up the monster bucket and looked imploringly at Denney.

Denney looked blearily over the top of her bright red reading glasses and added, "Kat, I don't have time for this. Besides, my contributions need to be *mine,* not *theirs,* " she said with a bit of theatrical flourish.

"Oh, all right," said Kat, with evident frustration, as she turned on her heel, grabbed her keys, and marched out the front door, purposely letting it slam behind her. She stomped across the front lawn to her car. She sometimes parked in front of the house at the curb because it was easier than using the alley and the garage. Besides, this made a noticeable statement of her level of annoyance.

Years ago, Kat had purchased an antique 1959 red Vespa Microcar, which was in excellent condition, to motor around the city when Denney didn't want to come along. She knew Denney would never ride in the Vespa. Denney told her she felt like a circus clown getting out of it, let alone into it. She thought it was just too small and humiliating.

Kat roared down St. James Court in her Vespa two-seater. The other seat was always full of something, so the fact that it wasn't Denney, wasn't a concern to her. Today her co-pilot was the big green bucket.

Chapter 4

Redemption in Bad Bones

Once in her car, Kat decided to swing by the Jeffersonian Club. She wasn't going to be forced by circumstances to fill the bucket first. She turned on her music to listen to Martha Redbone. Just as she pulled in front of the club, Martha finished singing "Underdog."

The sisters kept their membership, even though they used it less and less. The expense seemed unnecessary, and she intended to speak with Joseph, a highly esteemed member and influential black leader in the community, about the benefit of keeping it.

She walked into the heavily paneled, cherry anteroom looking for him. He had been a member since before the Book of Genesis and knew everything about the club, its history, and patrons. Joseph was talking with another member when she saw him. As she walked toward him, he turned his tall, patrician frame toward her. Her flip-flops slapped the marble floor, making a clicking sound that announced her arrival.

"Good morning, Joseph," Kat said lightly, "I hope I'm not interrupting, but do you have a minute for a short chat?"

"Why sure, Kathay." He excused himself from his conversation and, turning to her, said, "Let's have a quick toddy in the lounge, shall we?" Locally, they were known as Kat and Denney. Rarely were their given names used except by unusually formal persons, and then their names were often mispronounced by those who did not know them well. Between themselves, they referred to each other only by their given names for emphasis.

"Don't you think it's a little early? It's only eleven a.m.," Kat said with a wink, adding, "You know, you can call me Kat."

"He threw his head back and, with a hearty laugh, said, "*Kat*, you girls, when it comes to a toddy for the body, are like horses out of the gate," he said.

"I get your point," Kat said, smiling slyly as she craned her neck to look around the corner at the private and dimly lit bar. It was always nice and cool, a favorite spot to escape the heat of the day. It was also empty.

Joseph chuckled.

"Okay, let's." She was already feeling more relaxed.

"Good," Joseph replied softly, "as there is something I wish to share with you, too. It's about the Colonel." They settled into a booth near the bar. She ordered a Manhattan and Joseph a rum and Coke. As they waited, he leaned in and asked if she and Denney had been through the furniture in the carriage house since moving in.

She was puzzled. This was a random sort of question. "Well, as a matter of fact, Denney is doing that soon. Why do you ask?"

Joseph leaned back and looked away as if thinking about what to say next. He paused and smiled. "Several years ago, the Colonel called me to ask a favor. He had leased an apartment in New Orleans but decided to move on after a short time. So, he subleased the flat to a lady friend and left a desk in her safekeeping. Later, he argued with his landlady about a rent payment for that lady friend of his. He said he could prove he had paid the rent on her behalf, although the landlady alleged he had not. The landlady then said that she was going to sell the flat's contents for the back rent at auction through a place called Bypass Furniture and Auction. He called and asked me to buy the desk at auction and said he would pay me back no matter the cost. I was not comfortable with accepting this responsibility and did not agree."

Kat interrupted. "Why was a desk so important?" She had been contemplating her drink and slowly raised her head; with a fixed, appraising steady gaze, she asked, "Would it be possible that there could be something important enough in the desk that it could be of value to us?"

"Your Father could be a very devious and crafty individual. He didn't trust a lot of people and would hide important documents in the most unlikely places, telling few people where he may have hidden things," Joseph added. "So that's entirely likely."

"Returning to my story, he said he would find someone else to help him buy the desk. He never told me that he had, so I don't know if he followed through. He was no longer in a relationship with the lady friend, and she dropped off the map. However, he said that he would send other newly acquired pieces he owned in New Orleans back to Louisville. I believe those are the pieces in your carriage house that came from Bypass Furniture and Auction. I didn't say any more to him about it, and then he passed away. I can't believe it's been months now. I wanted you to have an opportunity to follow up at least."

Her brow furrowed as she finished her drink. "Wow, Joseph, we *will* follow up." They chatted for a few more minutes as they both finished their drinks. Kat retrieved the cherry from the bottom of her glass and said, "Thanks. It's always good seeing you."

As she slid out of the booth, Joseph smiled and answered, "Later, I trust."

Upon hearing Joseph's news about the Colonel, she had forgotten entirely what she would talk with him about. Now she needed to take care of something ugly and green. She would tell Denney about the furniture and the desk as soon as she got home.

Leaving the Jeffersonian Club, she roared down Broadway to the local hardware store. She would have much rather have been at the driving range with a bucket of practice balls. She was annoyed that she had to take time to fill that bucket. She approached a young man behind the sales counter. "Do you have any cheap crap, metal tools, available?"

He looked up from his phone and looked at Kat quizzically, "Yep, you must be familiar with our inventory. Follow me." He took her to a back shelf where there were plenty of flimsy metal tools and what-nots. She found a small level, a four-piece screwdriver set, with instructions, and to top it off; she found twelve, six-inch pieces of two-by-twos, a hammer, and a box of screws. She tossed all this into the bucket like she was collecting walnuts from the ground until it was full. Satisfied, and on her way to checkout, she noticed some small tape measures hanging from keyrings and tossed about six of them in as well. The clerk rang up her purchases, hardly containing his amusement.

As she settled back in her Vespa, she reached into her car organizer and found some delicately embossed thank-you notes. She pulled one out and hastily wrote on the inside, "You can thank me later." She put it into the matching envelope and slid it inside the bucket. Then she sped off to St. Kitts to drop it off.

Approaching the church, she noticed that parking was at a premium. The church lot was full of booths for the farmer's market and the street with shoppers. Muttering to herself how inconvenient this was, she looked for a spot on the street but found none. So, she pulled up in front of the church on the lawn. Fuming, she walked to the church to see where she should drop off the bucket. Upon reaching the imposing carved wooden doors of St. Kitts, she saw the church secretary, Mildred Purvis. Mildred's stout figure coming hurriedly out to meet her. Mildred immediately began to scold her for taking such license in parking.

Irritated, she spoke in a rush. "Kat, you know better! We're always replacing sod! People talk, you know, already such horrible things are said about your driving!"

Before Kat could say anything, Mildred quickly clasped her hands behind her ample back and stared at the green bucket, then at Kat. Mildred was taller than her and therefore Kat felt that she was always looking down at her as if in judgment.

"If you're here to drop off your bucket, the van left over an hour ago."

She set the bucket down, and dolefully looked at Mrs. Purvis. "What are you talking about? Vicar *Dick* assured me that the drop-off would be all day."

Mildred looked away and sighed.

"Is he taking competing medications again?" Kat asked sharply.

"Now you know that has happened only once this year!" Mildred said defensively. "He has been quite well for a long time. I know, why don't you take this down to the little shop called the Junk Bully? I'm sure they can use whatever you have in there." Mildred scooted the bucket back over to Kat with her foot, turned with military precision, and re-entered the church.

Knowing when she was defeated, Kat picked up the bucket, went to the Vespa, and pitched the bucket onto the car's passenger seat. Feeling somewhat remorseful about her parking skills she headed for the Junk Bully, only a mile away. As she pulled in front of the shabby, narrow shop, an exceedingly scruffy-looking man was leaning on a car outside.

The car couldn't have been worth more than $100, and she mused that it could fall apart if the guy kept leaning on it. As she pulled up, put the car in park, and rolled down her window, she hung the bucket outside. She looked up and down at the guy standing there. "Are you the head Bully around here?"

"I'm the chief executive officer; you might say," he replied.

"Here you go, my friend. Up at the church, they said you could use this." She dropped the bucket to the ground. It slapped the pavement with a boom, and a plume of gritty dust exploded into the air.

"You talkin' about that old guy, Vicar Dick?" he asked as he approached the Vespa.

"Absolutely," she said.

He picked up the bucket and noted a few bleary-eyed men pictured on the side. He recognized himself as one of the photo's unfortunates when he mumbled, "I will be no companion to such a misled and fantastical fellow!"

She recognized the quote from *The Pilgrim's Progress*, but she couldn't remember where she had heard it. Perhaps in a social study class or maybe a Bible study class, she thought.

Fearing he would give her back the bucket, she exclaimed, "Nevertheless, enjoy."

With a certain satisfaction, and now bucketless, she took that as her cue to pick up the pace. She popped a wheelie sending a plume of dust fender high and sped to the dog park, where she was supposed to meet Denney and the dogs.

Denney had already arrived at the park, unleashed the dogs, taken a seat on a bench, and poured drinks into two red plastic cups from her Van Gogh designer thermos. She handed one to Kat. The dogs were already frolicking like they owned the place.

Kat said, "Awesome, a Manhattan! I think it might help us find our inheritance. By the way, I talked with Joseph at the Jeffersonian Club today. He was acting mysterious and shared some interesting information. It concerns the old furniture in the carriage house and where it was bought in New Orleans. He said the Colonel might have hidden important papers in the furniture. He added something about a woman who subleased from the Colonel and a questionable buyer of a desk. We might not want to do anything with any old furniture for a while."

As she sipped from her red cup, she remembered Denney disliked having furniture with no known history— a peculiarity of hers. Denney often told Kat that one accepted all the bad bones of the owner or ill intentions, and their furniture soaked it up. Denney shuddered and replied, "You know how I dislike stray furniture, but I suspect the vicar might say there is redemption in even bad bones, eh?"

"You talkin' about Vicar Dick?" Kat asked. "You

know he is having trouble with competing medications again."

"Hmmm, I just hoped he was being mystical," mused Denney.

Chapter 5

The Kincaid Connection

That evening Denney thought about how little she knew about the Kincaids. Her Mother, Clarice Moore, came from a very wealthy family of bankers. After she left the Colonel and moved to New Orleans, no mention was made of the paternal Kincaids', including Sterling Kincaid, the sisters' father. She felt she knew more about her stepfather's family, the Carlyle's because she was around them for holidays and other events throughout her pre-teen and teenage life.

Denney only knew the Daggits from St. Kitts before her mother moved her and Kat to New Orleans, and then more recently, she and Kat transferred their membership to St. Kitts as adults. The Daggits had been stalwarts in the parish for generations. Her grandmother and grandfather, Julian and Mary Kincaid, were deceased, as was her mother. She tried to think of anyone who could fill in the history of her father's family.

As much as she hated the thought, Vicar Dick was the likely repository of much of that information. It wasn't that she disliked the Vicar, but conversations with him always seemed to devolve into gotcha sessions. Denney didn't know how it began; she just had that feeling and decided she would call the vicar in the morning and arrange a meeting.

After a restless night's sleep, Denney was up at five in the morning. She decided to fix her coffee early and leave a voice message on the vicar's office phone. Calling later and speaking to his administrative assistant, Mildred was a far more distasteful choice.

"This is Reverend Richard Roundtable. I'm away from my office at present; please leave a message at the tone." A brief beep signaled Denney to start talking.

"Dick, this is Denney Kincaid. I would very much like to sit down with you at your first opportunity and have a discussion. I believe you have my cell number. Thanks." Denney hung up the phone, glad she could accomplish this without personal interaction.

Denney stuck her cell phone into the pocket of her robe and took her coffee back to her bedroom. She was so tired that she laid her coffee cup on her nightstand and fell back to sleep.

A little more than two hours later, Kat called Denney, "Hey up there, breakfast is ready."

Denney did not feel appreciably better but rose and went downstairs.

Kat asked, "Are you okay? You sort of slept in."

"Oh, I didn't sleep well last night. I needed a little antihistamine and acid reducer between the post-nasal drip and the stomach acid meeting at various points in my throat. I took my coffee upstairs. I had only been up a short time when I dozed off again.

"I just wondered," Kat replied. "I saw someone used the Keurig, and it wasn't me."

"What do you remember about the Colonel's side of the family?"

"What? What brings this up?"

"It's the genealogy. I guess the 'genea' is out of the bottle now." We know that Mother's family was wealthy. She was able to leave us the home in New Orleans and a decent trust fund. Even Dr. Carlyle remembered us in his will. And, honestly, it's been enough to see us through till today, given our spending habits. I just find it difficult not to believe the Colonel was sitting on a bucket of gold when he passed. I know that sounds crass, but I can talk to you without parsing my words."

"I think you're right. Trying to pursue our inheritance is still a worthwhile use of our time," Kat responded. "I have some errands to run, and I'll be back later this morning."

Denny replied, "why don't you do that." She turned to go upstairs to her bedroom to change her clothes when her cell phone rang.

"Hello, this is Denney."

"Good morning. This is Vicar Dick. I listened to your voice mail, and if you'd like, we can meet this afternoon at one o'clock."

"Thanks, that's nice of you, vicar. Yes, I will see you

then."

"Very well, Denney, see you then."

Denney was relieved she could have this conversation so soon and perhaps be done with it. She decided to read the paper and water the garden before she left.

At promptly 12:55, Denney was on the porch of St. Kitts. She proceeded to Mildred's ante-office and greeted her.

"Good afternoon, Denney. The vicar said you were coming. Please go on in."

Mildred followed Denney as she walked into the Vicar's office. "Can I get you anything? Some water or perhaps some coffee?"

"Perhaps some water, please," responded Denney.

"The same," replied the vicar.

Denney thought how Mildred just loved to serve everyone. In this case, Denney felt she would be more comfortable with a glass of water to fool with rather than her reading glasses since she didn't smoke or knit, and she was a bit uncomfortable.

"It's good to see you, Denney. I meant to thank you for your gift to cover the sod repair in front of the church."

"No need to thank me, I wanted to do it. But that's not why I'm here."

"I surmised as much from your message. I could hear some anxiety in your voice. I discovered an old baptismal record which surprised me. Was that why you called me?"

"I was wondering how much you knew about the Kincaid family?"

Just then, Mildred entered with a tray and two glasses of water. She handed Denney a paper doily and another to the vicar. "For under the water glass," she explained, then gave them their water.

"Thanks, Mildred, we are all set now," gently indicating that Mildred could leave.

As Mildred left, she closed the door behind her.

Vicar Dick smiled and said, "Okay, where were we? Oh yes, the Kincaids."

"Yes, but actually, it has more directly to do with the Colonel."

Vicar Dick's expression turned a little more serious. "Of course, what would you like to know?"

"Considering what I don't know, that is a huge question. What can you tell me about him? After Mother took us to New Orleans, we rarely saw Father. We came here for a week or two on a few summer breaks, but he had us enrolled in programs during the day. We joined him for dinner, always at the Jeffersonian Club. A day or so before we left, he would take us shopping, which was about it. I don't remember much about St. Kitts from before Mother moved us. I know you weren't the Rector then."

The Vicar looked a bit stunned. "I'm sorry, Denney. Of course, I knew your father. And I will share what I know. I guess I wasn't expecting your question. He took a breath and began. "So, where to start. We met when I was an assistant here at St. Kitts. Being about the same age, we got along quite well. I was eager for a friend my age as I knew no one when I accepted the position here. And, yes, the Jeffersonian was quite his stomping ground. He invited me there quite often and always picked up the tab for our dinner and drinks. He wouldn't hear of it otherwise. He had a quick wit and loved to debate politics and religion. He said he believed in God but only came to St. Kitts on Sunday morning to appease your Grandparents. I think he understood my position on the church and spirituality, and I felt I was truly making headway in this regard with him, although I knew he would never admit it. He was a bit rakish and sometimes, I'm afraid, a bit callous.

I asked him to mentor a couple of the older boys in the youth group because your father was fun to be around, and I thought it might be good for all involved. But he just wasn't going to be tied down. Don't get me wrong; he was generous and amusing; however, he didn't want responsibility for anyone else. If you were with him, then fine, but he wasn't going to seek anyone out.

Then I was called to a position as rector of another parish out of state. We stayed in touch for a while, and he said he would visit, but he never did. He continued working with your grandfather, managing the restaurant businesses.

When your mother left him, he told me he felt no kinship to this place and wanted to see the world. I would receive postcards and occasionally a brief note from him from all over the place. Mostly islands, as I recall. He told me in one of his notes he would never marry again but sure was having fun.

Your grandparents, the Kincaids, came to me and were beside themselves, but they supported him in whatever he wanted to do. They said they kept hoping he would find himself."

"I'm wondering," said Denney, "did you ever keep any of these postcards or notes?"

"Funny, I may have, but I don't even know where they would be now," said the vicar. "I tell you what, if I find one, I'll be sure to give it to you."

"Did you ever meet up with him again?"

"Yes, for a while. The Colonel moved back to Louisville for a couple of years when your grandparents became ill. He lived with them in the house you are now in and made sure they were well-cared for.

Your Grandfather Kincaid passed first and then, about a year later, your Grandmother. He inherited the house and stayed on for a bit over a year. He was instrumental in my return to St. Kitts. I was told he joined the Vestry to have a say in bringing me back. I am ever so grateful for that.

Soon thereafter, he'd leave for months at a time. He would stay somewhere for weeks or months, then leave. Oddly, he started sending a piece of furniture here and there to store in his carriage house. I had a key for a while and would open the doors for the delivery folks. On his last return home, he again invited me to the Jeffersonian for dinner and a drink. He even called Joseph to join us. What a night. That was the last time I saw him before he died.'' Then the vicar said, "I'm sorry, Denney, did I ramble on too much?"

"Oh no, I was listening to every word. If you recall anything, you think I might like to know, please call me."

"I will, Denney. And you stop by any time," he added.

Denney rose to leave, and the vicar did too. They both nodded to each other as Denney left.

The Vicar sat down in his desk chair and swiveled to better see through his window as Denney exited and walked down the front steps. He continued watching well past the time she was out of sight.

He remembered more, of course, but thought it was better not to share everything at once. His mind went to Winfield Daggit, the son of a prominent local family, who seemed troubled even as a boy. He could see it as clearly as if it were yesterday. Winfield was mesmerized with the Colonel even when he was in the grade school Sunday School classes. When Winfield was eighteen and home from boarding school, the Daggits would insist the family attend church together. The vicar felt Winfield was modeling himself after the Colonel to some degree, but then he only saw him for an hour each Sunday.

After church one morning, the vicar called to the Colonel and asked to talk to him. "You know, there are two young men here that I think need some help from a person, who like you, could show them life can be fun. They are both so serious. Their names are Tony Perez and Winfield Daggit.

He could recall so clearly the Colonel looking at him and saying, "I don't know the Perez kid, and I barely know Winfield." The vicar pleaded with him to help, especially with Winfield. "I fear Winfield is becoming very serious and is pushing people away. You know you're related, if distantly, to Winfield.

The Colonel just said, "I'll see about it," wished him a good afternoon, and left.

The vicar shuddered as he remembered the Colonel's help going awry. But why should he be surprised? He had been like that with his wife and daughters.

Chapter 6

Footwear

The day came and went for the girls. Denney finished her script review for the little playhouse group, and Kat no longer had to find a repository for her generosity. It was smooth sailing into Friday and the start of the weekend.

Friday morning, Denney bustled around the kitchen in bright pink yoga pants, a pink top, and pink shoes. She softly hummed while warming some biscotti to go with her and Kat's morning coffee. She knew her sister got up early to walk at least four miles before the start of her day.

Denney liked to do some light yoga stretches but was not interested in sweating. They both had bought an abundance of workout clothes to help them keep up an interest in exercising when shopping together. Denney had to allow that while Kat was much more disciplined, Denney could relish the fact that she was much more stylish.

As she nibbled on her biscotti, she thought frustrating their coffee time had been rushed the other morning due to that damn bucket. She liked ritual, and it was unsettling to her when interruptions occurred. Well, she would talk to Kat about it over cocktails at the carriage house this evening.

She also wanted to talk to Kat about the old furniture in the carriage house that either needed to go or stay. They could use some free money and needed to keep that in mind should there be no inheritance. She also realized the sale of this furniture would be a drop in the bucket either way they went. After all, the fabric on the sofa and chairs in the main house seemed a little warm for this climate during the summer and needed to be lightened up.

She hated to have to concern herself with how to pay for these things. This was certainly not how she had envisioned herself at this time of her life. She found it to be tedious and exhausting. So, she decided this was a great opportunity to look over the odd pieces of furniture in the carriage house, as one glance back at the old furniture in the main house convinced her it had to be spiffed up.

Denney called to Kat, "Make your way to the front porch."

Kat ambled down the staircase and directly to the front porch. The aroma of fresh biscotti and brewed coffee was tantalizing as it drifted through the morning air ahead of her. She loved the fragrance of fresh coffee and warm biscotti lingering in the morning air. She would often comment that life was grand in these instances.

After their coffee, the girls eased into the afternoon. Kat grabbed her most recent crime novel and took all three dogs to the dog park to play, admonishing Denney not to take any action on the furniture yet. They had to consider what Joseph had told them. Ever aware of Denney's bizarre belief about previously owned personal property, she acquiesced that it stood to reason to Denney that one should choose carefully when collecting or discarding an item. In this case, the Colonel's furniture had come with the carriage house.

While Kat was gone, Denney proceeded over the brick walkway to the rear of the property. She unlocked the door of the carriage house and was immediately welcomed by its stuffiness. She hurriedly opened the windows. The rooms, when opened, were usually breezy except for July and August. There was no breeze today. It was just plain muggy in there, even though the unceasing drone of the ceiling fan did its best to create a quasi-livable space.

She looked at each piece of furniture. There were at least five large pieces that had no character and were just boring. Nothing was hidden in any of them. So why keep them? She would sell them. She thought it was very uncharacteristic of the Colonel to have owned these pieces. He was known for his flair—not a theatrical flair—but like the liquor commercial promoting the most interesting man in the world.

She knew he wasn't *that* man but could have known *that* man and would have spent some time at his bar, then moved on after buying some interesting item commemorating spending time with *that* guy.

She shook her head as if to release this wandering, random voice, closed the windows, locked the door, and walked quickly back to the main house.

Kat had returned from the dog park covered with paw prints. "Look, Denney! The water fountain was overflowing and made such a muddy mess! Twelve dog paws splashing through mud just to have a drink!"

"Did you clean their paws before you let them in the house?" Denney sighed. "I just can't keep mopping."

Kat called the dogs and checked their paws as requested. Most of the mud had been dispatched somewhere between the last grassy area at the park and her car seats.

"Yes, Cinderella, the paws pass muster. I'm going to clean up, then let's go shopping. I want to stop by that new Shoe Emporium." Kat knew Denney loved to look at all types of footwear and would never object. The small store had just opened on Oak Street and was within walking distance. Kat liked to support small businesses and get to know the owners.

"That sounds great. Let me just change into something fun," Denney responded.

At the Emporium, Kat found a pair of solid black cross-trainers, located her size, and was ready to leave when she saw Denney sitting on a small stool with five boxes piled in front of her.

"All these lovely shoes, I can't decide," sighed Denney. Finally, she chose some pink Sketchers to go with her new pink yoga outfit.

Kat was amused as she watched Denney hold the shoes up to the light and inspect the stitching, the soles, and the grommets for the laces. Then she held them up to the pink yoga outfit she was wearing.

"Don't you already have pink?" quizzed Kat.

"Probably, but that's what I'm wearing, and they seem worn now." Denney shot back. "Yes, these will work nicely." Denney nodded approvingly as she removed her reading glasses.

As they left the shoe store, Denney asked, "Kat, what did you buy?"

Kat clutched the box under her arm and ignored her question.

"Well, what did you get?"

"Oh, I got a pair of cross-trainers that will go with a lot of my exercise clothes," Kat replied warily.

Denney grabbed the box from Kat's poorly secured grip and opened it. Under the tissue paper were hideous black athletic shoes. The shoes were almost high-top, and the laces began at the toe and continued up the center of the shoe to the edge of the tongue. She shuddered at the lack of attractiveness. "So, Kat, are you going lipstick or lumberjack? Shall I call you Spike? That's the *only* explanation! Please, just DO NOT get a nose ring!"

Kat grabbed her box and stated severely, "These damn shoes cost $250 bucks!"

Denney froze. "We don't have the money for that!"

"I don't give a shit," huffed Kat and off she walked.

Denney bent down to pick up the tissue paper that had fallen from the box to the sidewalk. At least there would be some savings in reusing it, perhaps relining her lingerie drawer. Denney caught up with Kat at the liquor store and found her pulling various bottles of expensive gin off the shelf. Denney scolded, "Since when did we start drinking gin, Spike?"

Kat snapped back, "First it's the shoes, now it's my choice in liquor," as she slammed the bottles on the counter to pay. She turned to look at Denney and said, "So I choose your plastic." Then she grabbed the bagged gin and stomped out of the store, a plastic bag of clanging bottles brushing her thighs.

The cashier rolled her eyes and looked at Denney. Denney, left to pay for the gin, looked at the clerk, and sighed. "She's such a little snot. I'll make sure those are her early Christmas presents for her rehab group." Once outside, she leaned against the sill of the store's front window and clumsily changed into her new Sketchers. Pleased with her selection, she pointed each toe and moved each foot from side to side to inspect them for the walk home.

As Denney approached home and the front porch, she saw Kat slumped in one of the wicker chairs with gin bottles listing in the bag at her feet. It had been a long afternoon, and this was to be their time to talk, but conversation just now was awkward.

"There's nothing more gagging than warm gin, Spike. If you're going to drink that toilet water, you need to take it indoors." She dramatically tossed her hair to punctuate her quip when she noticed an empty liquor bag at the curb. With some apparent self-righteousness, she headed for the street to pick it up. As she made her way over the lawn, the sprinklers tripped. "Crap!" she shouted. Now, dancing around to save her new shoes, she finally reached the porch with the dripping plastic bag. Her shoes were covered in grass clippings and mud. Her hair was flat and damp.

Kat looked at her and started laughing. "Here, you take the gin in—it looks more like it belongs to you now."

Denney removed her new sodden Sketchers and tossed them into the soggy liquor bag. As she passed the outdoor rubbish bin, she muttered to herself about a good walk spoiled and how she detested being barefoot. Then she tossed the bag and shoes into the trash.

Kat made her way to the porch on the side of the carriage house for their evening cocktails while Denney repaired herself. Rusty was running and jumping in the backyard with Gus and Jules when he spied her and came running excitedly, full tilt, to greet her.

Thank God Rusty is not a piddler. So many cockers had this tendency when excited. Her friends who had this breed would put up with pee-sodden shoes and thought it was endearing. Not so with Rusty. He could put a cork in it under the most excitable situations. She sat down in one of the Adirondack chairs with Rusty at her feet.

Denney had dried herself and was finally laughing at the afternoon. Kat could tell she was ready to sip cocktails and close the week with conversation.

"Kat, shouldn't we just get rid of some of the oddball pieces of furniture in the carriage house? I think we just sell them."

Denney studied her. "I just wanted to say I missed being able to talk with you the other morning due to the bucket thing." She was sincere and offered this observation kindly.

Kat thought about the afternoon and how crazy life could get.

"I hear you, Denney. It's important to me too—that we communicate," Kat said warmly. "Let's not do the bucket ever again, okay?"

Denney smiled back. "Thank you, Jesus."

Kat replied, "Let's just donate the gin to the farmer's market next weekend and consider it part of our pledge."

Chapter 7

A Big Damp Man

On Saturday morning, over coffee on the front porch, Denney was busy on her laptop. She was looking up flights to New Orleans. Her computer was on her lap, and her coffee cup was on the table beside her. Kat came to join her, with the dogs rustling along after. "Nice of you to join me this morning," Denney quipped.

"Ahh, the first volley has been shot over the bow," responded Kat. She plopped down in her wicker chair with her latte in hand and studied her sister. There was some resemblance between them, but mostly in their reddish-brown hair color. She was told how uncanny it was their hair color remained the same over fifty years. Everyone commented on it. She would tell everyone it was genetics.

While neither was tall or big-boned, Denney had picked up some weight over the past thirty years. A pound a year or so, Denney often lamented. Twenty pounds was not easy for her to lose either. Denney would often remark her metabolism really could use a jump start. Kat would listen sympathetically as Denney described how her internist told her that her thyroid was under control and he wouldn't adjust her prescription. She knew he was a chronic liar.

Kat, on the other hand, did a lot of yard work and exercise. She didn't mind sweating either, so her weight was not a problem. She could look a bit dehydrated though, so she drank copious amounts of water so she wouldn't wrinkle like a prune.

She noticed Denney was immersed in her computer, stopping only for a sip of coffee now and then. Breaking the silence, she addressed her, "What 'cha doing over there?"

"I'm looking for flights to New Orleans, dear. I found one for us, and I am going to book now," replied Denney. "Since we agreed the carriage house furniture was no good to us, that leaves the desk that our father seemed to care so much about. We know it was in New Orleans because Joseph said it had been in the possession of some woman there. He also told us the carriage house furniture was sent from Beau Buford's Bypass Furniture and Auction. So, let's check out Buford's place for the desk when we get there."

"Oh, okay. What are we looking at?"

"We will leave in three days, mid-afternoon arrival in New Orleans. We can open the house there and look into the news from Joseph." Denney finished her booking and asked Kat about her disbursement of the bucket.

"About that. I ended up taking it to this place called the Junk Bully."

Denney asked, "Where is that? I can't place it."

"You know that old concrete block building with the faded green paint about a mile north of the church," Kat said.

"Why would you know of that place?" quizzed Denney.

"Mildred sent me there. Anyway, the guy who runs the place seems to know Vicar Dick. At one point, I also think he may have been in trouble with the law. I can tell you this: he has a blonde afro that's big enough to park a school bus in. It's fascinating to watch it sway when he walks around. You really should visit sometime."

"Seriously?" Denney, who fancied herself something of a behaviorist, said thoughtfully, "Perhaps when we get back."

***

On Sunday, the sisters walked to church. The weather was glorious and not too hot. The streets lined with trees and thick overhanging branches of green shaded their morning stroll—the *Book of Common Prayer* firmly in their hands.

"What possesses us to choose the 10:45 service in summer?" Denney inquired thoughtfully. Then answering her question, she said, "I know! There is no music in the 8:15, and it is ever so dreary."

To which Kat added, "Oh, look, new sod out front."

As they approached the narthex of St. Kitts Episcopal Church, Ashleigh Daggit called to them, "Kathaaaaaay, Lyndeeeen, hurry not."

The sisters froze in their tracks. Denney lowered her sunglasses and looked over the top at Ashleigh. As it was often her nature to offer correction, while many times misunderstood, she said, "Mr. Daggit, need I remind you once again of the proper pronunciation of my dear sister's name and my own," she imperiously replied. "Perhaps a story will help you remember. Kathay was named for Cathay, the older and certainly more poetic name for what we now know as the country of China. I was named for the Linden tree, with its heart-shaped leaves and cheery, beautifully fragrant yellow blooms. The twist on the spelling and the silent "e" at the end of my name bespeaks our family's natural inclination toward drama. Now, does that help you picture why you are mispronouncing our names and how much richer the experience would be for you if you did not?"

Ashleigh, speechless but not wounded, stood in front of the sisters with sweat running down the sides of his clean-shaven round face onto his starched white collar. His shaggy head of brown hair was always clean but without the benefit of a good haircut. His most striking feature was his big sky-blue eyes.

Kat couldn't help but feel a little bad for Ashleigh as he could never get the hang of looking well-kept. He was a heavy man, at least seventy pounds overweight, his clothes were ill-fitting, and his shirt was always coming out of his pants in the back. He was of average height. Ashleigh never wore a suit because he said the heat was just too intolerable for that. He was just a big damp man for the most part.

While Kat often felt a little sorry for him because he

tried so hard and appeared foolish in his attempt to gain attention, she knew that at times Denney could grow very impatient with the man. However, Denney never made fun of him as so many others did. He was short on social graces even though he belonged to the Daggit family, one of the wealthiest families around.

Ashleigh confided in the sisters that he felt beloved by them. Kat wondered at the basis for this and assumed he remained as close to them as was allowed. She could not help but laugh at the whole scene that had unfolded before her and inquired kindly, "Ashleigh, tell us what's on your mind."

Ashleigh looked at Denney for permission to speak.

"Proceed, Ashleigh," Denney pronounced as she sighed heavily.

"Did you not get a notice?" Ashleigh exclaimed. "I was told you did."

Denney was now thoroughly exasperated, "Speak clearly, man, and tell us precisely. What notice?"

As sweat rings deepened under his arms, Ashleigh placed his hands on his hips. As he stood there, other parishioners gave him a wide berth. "A notice in the mail awaits you about a package for you at the post office," he declared with a bit of anxiety.

"We received no notice," Denney stated impatiently. "Oh wait, maybe that was what Rusty had in his mouth a couple of days ago." Looking hard at Kat, Denney quickly pointed out Rusty's paper-eating habit and the dire consequences of acute constipation waiting on their doorstep should he persist in his perverse practice.

Kat turned to Ashleigh. "Please put your arms down as the breeze is beginning to pick up." The pungent smell of sweat without the benefit of a good deodorant was beginning to envelop the space. Ashleigh dropped both his arms to only raise his hand from the waist to speak.

Denney speared Ashleigh with her gaze. "Must you?"

Sweat poured down Ashleigh's back, over his collar, and around his waist as he became more excited and anxious over his next proposal. "I would be ever so glad to retrieve the package and drop it by for you."

"Absolutely not," chorused the sisters.

Once Ashleigh was on their doorstep, he would sit on one of their porch chairs. He would sweat profusely, stink up the chair, and all would be lost until cushions could be replaced.

Kat hastily added, "Thanks for the offer, but we're going out of town, so I'll pick it up tomorrow."

Ashleigh looked crestfallen.

She immediately sensed his disappointment. "Really, Ashleigh, it was kind of you to offer, but not necessary."

Ashleigh brightened up as the sisters moved on. They didn't give Ashleigh any further consideration as they didn't want to participate in a conversation with him about their private affairs. Over time, they had found him to be much too open and guileless. He would share any information he had with anyone.

After the service, Kat turned to Denney as they walked toward home, cutting through the side church lot to avoid the front lawn and comments about the new sod.

"Denney, are you packed and ready to go?" Kat asked.

Denney had considered what she would pack for a trip of unknown duration. It was too late to order a sleek little black travel dress from the catalogs and too hot to wear one anyway. What was in her closet would have to do. She responded rather resignedly, "Yes, as much as possible, I am packed to go." She still coveted that little black dress but also knew that after the plane flight, no matter how short a duration in the sky, her ankles would balloon up and spoil the effect anyway.

"How about you, Kat?"

"Pants and shirts, that's it for me," said Kat. "Are we taking swimsuits?"

"Swimsuits? Really? You know we don't wear swimsuits in public at our age."

"What do you think we should swim in? Capris?"

"For a woman in her fifties, have you no shame?" Do you think others wouldn't gawk? I always knew you were raised early on in a Soviet orphanage and just came into our parents' life by luck, and perhaps a good heart on their part. I believe it accounts for your lack of self-awareness," she said with a twinkle in her eye.

Kat replied, "It's too bad you can only get collagen in your cheekbones. Just think what a full-body collagen treatment might do."

"Do they offer that?" Denney's eyes lit up with hope.

"Fuck no, Lindene!"

The sisters laughed together and walked arm and arm home to their beloved dogs and their last night of the weekend.

Chapter 8

A Freaky Parrot

"I'm going to run by the post office and perhaps visit Merriweather," Kat announced as she grabbed her car keys and ran out the back door with Rusty.

"Don't forget the package," Denney called out behind her.

Denney took care of closing the main house and contacting Carmen, their dog sitter. Carmen and her family were longtime friends. Carmen's mother and father had emigrated from Cuba when it was possible for them both to do so. Their church sponsor had settled them in Florida. Later they moved to Louisville for Carmen's father to accept a promotion. They found a house that was near St. Kitts and began attending services. Carmen's father spoke English well, but her mother needed help transitioning and could not drive.

Mildred Purvis, the church secretary, had jumped right in and "adopted" the family. Carmen and her brother were then teens and had perfected their English quickly. Kat and Denney involved them in the youth activities and often took them to the mall to shop. Over time the sisters became adopted aunts to Carmen and close friends to the family.

Carmen always stayed in the carriage house with the dogs while the sisters were away. She had access to the main house, but she said she preferred the smaller, more private carriage house where she had her room and bath.

Denney made a mental note to replenish her candy stash so it would be ready and waiting for her when she returned. Most of the candies had been partially consumed and then lovingly rewrapped, as was her fashion. They were a little fuzzy. She knew that Kat thought she should just replace the whole lot but knew that she would not do so. Kat had even accused her of being worse than a serial killer with souvenirs. She knew this ritual had become a necessary part of her life and consoled herself by thinking, "The Captain is on the bridge." Therefore, because she knew she was in command, she did not worry about petty habits. Kat was her officer of the watch, an able seaman, and could pilot if required.

There wasn't anything left to do. Denney felt exhausted and waited on the front porch for Carmen's arrival. Gus and Jules reclined on the cool porch at her feet while she drank her sweet tea with a mint leaf secured with ice at the bottom of her glass.

* * *

Kat was in the post office while Rusty waited patiently in the passenger seat of the Vespa. He hadn't wanted to enter the post office and greet his human friends this morning. His focus appeared to be laser-sharp on the passenger window. He was staring down the road to where

Mrs. Merriweather lived and where he always was given the little McDonald's creamers, she saved for him.

Kat returned to the car with a rather large manila envelope taped securely closed. There was no return address. She threw it on the passenger floorboard and sped on to Mrs. Merriweather's. As they got closer to their destination, Rusty's little butt started twitching with anticipation.

Upon reaching Mrs. Merriweather's house, Kat and Rusty hopped out of the car and were greeted at the front door by Peter, a freaky big parrot who was demented and neurotic. He knew only a few short sentences. He did not like dogs, as he had been chased by an impressively large greyhound when he was young and had never fully recovered. Kat thought he could use an extended stay in some avian trauma program.

After entering the foyer, Peter flew to the drapes as Mrs. Merriweather ushered Kat and Rusty into her front parlor. The bird shrieked, "Shit, shit, get the dog, get the dog!"

Kat figured that must have been what Mrs. Merriweather said when she was chasing the greyhound. They sat on the sofa and drank coffee with a good portion of Captain Morgan's rum swirled into each cup. The little creamers were nestled in a bowl, ready to be opened for Rusty.

Rusty eyed the little bowl with anticipation and decided to lie down directly under Peter. Kat tried to scooch him over, but Rusty was not moving. Peter had settled on the room's highest point—the curtain rod, cocked his head and stared fixedly at Rusty. Kat asked Mrs. Merriweather why Peter was off his perch.

Mrs. Merriweather casually replied, "Oh is he, dear? I hadn't noticed."

She pointed to Peter at the top of the curtain. "Isn't that Peter?"

Mrs. Merriweather looked up and then over at Kat. "I daresay he's not coming down now, so we should just continue our visit, dear."

"Sure," said Kat.

Peter looked stressed, perched on the curtain rod but out of range.

Kat eased back in her chair and worked on her second rum and coffee.

Mrs. Merriweather was on her third and feeling chatty.

"I heard some small talk and wondered if you know anything about the Daggit family," asked Kat.

Merriweather hiccupped and placed her cup on her saucer. "Well, dear, the family is rich. Mrs. Daggit was a kind soul, as I remember. Oh, and I believe there were twin boys."

"Who told you that?"

"Oh, I don't remember, it was a long time ago. I do believe it to be true, though."

Kat was unable to question her further because Peter,

in his continued distress, had a minor bowel explosion, which landed right on the white spot on top of Rusty's head. Unknowingly, Mrs. Merriweather reached over to pat Rusty. She quickly withdrew her hand. "Looks like Petey pooped."

As Kat poured herself some more coffee and rum, she gazed fondly over at Rusty, who was asleep, his nose capped off with a little empty coffee creamer. He was snoring rather loudly. They decided to let it go for now and added a little more rum to their coffees.

Kat redirected Mrs. Merriweather to her statement about Ashleigh.

"As I think back, I recall the Colonel passed that on to me by simply asking in a conversation whether I knew there were two Daggit boys, twins as I recall. You know Ashleigh, but the other brother left town a long time ago, and no one has heard from him as far as I know."

Mrs. Merriweather and Kat decided to dispense with the coffee and just have another round of rum.

"Can you remember anything else from your conversation with the Colonel?"

"Oh dear, no, not another thing," Merriweather added. "If I do remember any more, I will call you."

Kat concluded that at this point in their beverage consumption, what Merriweather could or couldn't recall was academic. She finished her last bit of rum and scooped Rusty up to bundle him out to the car. Kat and Merriweather hugged each other goodbye, and Rusty got another pat, but this one was to his hindquarters. Peter screeched and shouted, "Damn dog."

Kat realized that driving home in her condition was probably not the best idea she ever had. She considered walking but felt a bit wobbly. She tried to close her eyes and take a nap, but the Vespa was too snug. Twist and turn as she might, there was no comfortable napping position. In the end, she called Denney.

Perturbed, Denney backed the Mark V out of the garage, into the alley, and cautiously made her way to Merriweather's. The car was *huge*. It was a land yacht, three thousand feet long, and had only two doors. The Bill Blass Edition, Lincoln Mark V. It was blue on white with a Landau vinyl roof, opera windows, chamois leather seats, and a Cartier clock that didn't work.

Kat was sitting on Merriweather's stoop, watching for her arrival.

As Denney pulled to the curb, Kat walked toward her. Denney reached across the passenger seat and pushed open the door, calling to Rusty, "Come on, my sweet puppy, and bring that old sot with you."

Rusty bounded into the car and snuggled next to her on the huge bench seat. Kat fell into the remaining part of the front seat and blearily eyed Rusty, saying, "You little traitor!"

By the time they arrived home, it was early evening. Kat clumsily stepped out of the Mark V, hiccupped, and called to Rusty. He stretched and slowly walked over to her. She cradled a sleepy Rusty in her arms as she swayed across the backyard.

Carmen met them at the back door. She gathered Rusty in her arms, inspected his head, and remarked, "Looks like you've been to Merriweather's house, Kat." Kat smiled as Carmen cuddled Rusty and softly spoke Spanish in his ear.

Kat made it to the front porch where Denney waited and had placed her Manhattan on the table next to her chair. She considered she might have to forgo tonight's nightcap.

There they watched as evening descended and talked while Carmen's soft voice came from the kitchen as she cleaned off Rusty's head.

"We leave early tomorrow morning, Kat. Perhaps you need a good night's sleep," said Denney.

Kat giggled to herself that bourbon plus rum was not a good sum. She figured that she was overdue for bed.

"True dat, Lindene. See ya in the morning."

Chapter 9

Don't Use the Plane Toilet

Tuesday morning came, and the girls were off to the airport. Kat had taken a couple of aspirin and drunk at least twenty-four ounces of water before retiring. She assured Denney she felt sparkling.

They were excited to be on their way to their home on Phillip Street in the Garden District of New Orleans. Once seated, Denney leaned forward and gazed out the window while the city below took on the appearance of a game board. Then turning to Kat, she asked, "Do you remember our first plane ride to New Orleans?"

"Of course! Remember, Mother told us not to use the plane toilet?"

Denney smirked. "That warning follows me to this day! But I mean *being* in New Orleans."

Kat looked far away. "We didn't know why Mother moved us there at first as pre-teens, did we? The Colonel only visited us a couple of times, and then we visited him during the summer."

"It's a good thing we found out about the divorce, or

Dr. Carleton's house visits would have been *tres* awkward," Denney added.

Denney reclined her chair and asked, "Kat, what do you most remember about growing up in New Orleans?"

"I will never forget Mother talking about her debutante days in Louisville. She had her choice of men, according to her, but she fell hard for our father. I also remember Aunt Sal said she appeared quite the proper lady. Still, she enjoyed the bad boys, and the Colonel fit the bill as he was handsome, wealthy, intelligent, and, yes, fairly oppositional. Unfortunately, his moodiness became more tedious than charming. I suppose the specter of beginning anew intrigued her. I always thought she impulsively bought the house on Phillip Street."

"Remember, when she first met Carleton, the plastic surgeon, once in New Orleans and among a new crowd?"

Sure, I remember," said Denney. "She said they met at a neighborhood party, but I know I always thought she was his patient. Didn't you?"

When their mother passed, she left the house on Phillip Street to both daughters. Kat moved into the house immediately, but Denney, married, stayed in New York City."

"Yeah, it took a while to leave the shit sandwich but then I moved in with you as we had so often talked about," added Denney.

The rest of the flight was uneventful. Kat read, and Denney wanted to nap.

"Kat, I just can't keep my eyes open, but you know how I am about falling asleep in public transportation. Please don't let me snore, will you?"

"Sure. I've got your six, sis." Kat was reading a detective novel and often picked up the vocabulary.

Given the heat, the arrival in New Orleans and the taxi ride to their home were pleasant enough.

Kat and Denney loved the Phillip Street house, now their second home. Kat had been ecstatic when Denney decided to leave her relationship and come to New Orleans to share this home with her. She was hopeful that the marksmanship classes that Denney took when she arrived were just to blow off some steam and not to whack her most recent shit sandwich.

After their mother died, Kat moved in and did not renovate—always hopeful that Denney would come and do the job so Kat could play more golf. She had put money aside for this possibility as she was quite a good gambler and had won a very substantial amount at the casino. Kat was quite happy when Denney undertook the renovation. She asked her to design a working fireplace in the kitchen, even though it probably wouldn't be used. The ambiance was enough reason.

Denney had undertaken the renovation with gusto. Brick walls were exposed along the rear wall. She had included a door to a small porch and a brick walkway to the kitchen herb garden. She installed a bay window on the other side of the island so they both could take their small meals there if they wished to do so. There was plenty of light in this room.

A coffee bar on the counter was always ready for use with aromatic beans and Kat's foam machine. A butler's pantry behind the fireplace stored necessities that would rival the Windsor Hotel for choices of expensive liquor. Big ceiling fans were everywhere. All in all, it was a spectacular-looking decor.

Mid-morning, Denney strolled into the living room with her coffee in one hand and her warm biscotti in the other. She had spared no expense on this room. With its painted wainscoting and beautiful wooden floors, this room was more traditional, with modern pastel upholstered furniture.

The furniture was exceptionally comfortable, very "cushiony," she would say. The fireplace was non-working but left for the decor as it had a smashingly pretty mantel.

She had installed pocket doors to the hallway and to the dining room. All were beautiful wood, and she made sure they stayed in working order. Pale pastel Persian rugs on the floors added beautiful color—otherwise, a neutral palette in furniture.

Art was everywhere, with lovely pieces on the sofa table and behind the couch. Some of the art the sisters collected and some of it was left by their mother. Lamps were antique but worked with the more modern furniture because the sisters both had excellent eclectic taste.

Denney padded upstairs to her bedroom to get ready for the day. They would have to forgo their morning ritual as they had too much to do. She was all right with this decision because she had made it. She entered her bedroom and placed her coffee on top of the dresser.

This room was her favorite. Her bedroom was grand in scale and amazing to look at. Cherry Queen Anne style double bed with the best mattress money could buy. The dresser had a beveled mirror and held crystal perfume bottles and a lovely small lamp. The comfortable plush white upholstered chair with ottoman waited for her in the evenings as she often read her emails here, "running the traps," she would say. A bench was at the end of the bed and would invariably hold a small stack of swaths of expensive material.

All plush white bedding adorned her bed. Teal and gray accents in pillows and lamps with soft light, plush area rugs graced the room. She configured a walk-in closet which took away some space from the room, but that was okay. The bath next to her room had opened to adjoin the bedroom.

Feeling comfortable and now sleepy, she climbed into bed under the plush covers. Gus was already there, warm and cozy. Jules, at the side of the bed, fell asleep quickly and was snoring lightly.

Chapter 10

Brubeck and Beer

Kat opened the garage door where her dark cherry Electric EW 29 Electric Trike with the rear basket was parked. She hopped on and headed out to the neighborhood market to shop for beer and munchies she would need for the first week or so. Denney had reminded her about cocktails at six p.m. before she left, so she was on a mission of sorts.

"I'll have some brie and fruit too, so don't snack around too much, Kat," cautioned Denney.

"Sounds fine. I'll see you in a bit." Kat took off on the trike, wearing a helmet and goggles.

When she arrived at her favorite market, she loaded up her basket and went to the cooler, where there was an excellent selection of beer. She was very fond of Guinness beer. She looked around but could not find her brew in the case. She spotted the store owner and asked, "Hey, Mike, what did you do with my beer?"

"Oh, you're back," Mike said dourly. "Unfortunately, you are about the only one that buys it around here, so I had to stop stocking it."

"Well, just kill me and feed me to the poor," Kat wailed.

"There is no need to retire to your fainting couch just yet. You can go to the grocery store and pick some up there. It's not too far away."

Kat spun around and said, "OKAY, I'm riding my motorized trike and can't navigate too fast in traffic. Are you telling me I can get there without having to negotiate traffic and keep my groceries from going bad?"

"What I'm telling you is, they have the beer. I know how you drive, and I am not telling you how to do that. I can watch your groceries if you want, and you can pick them up on the way back. How about that?"

Kat considered this for a moment and responded, "Great, can you keep them cold, though?"

"Sure," said Mike, all the while smiling and shaking his head.

Kat left the groceries and took off for the beer run. She pulled up the location on her phone and noticed there were sidewalks almost all the way there. Not one to care about unclear rules, she plowed her way down the sidewalk, ignoring the complaints of pedestrians. She couldn't understand them anyway because she had her earbuds in and was listening to Dave Brubeck.

Kat parked on the sidewalk outside the store, jogged inside, spied the beer case, and grabbed a six-pack of Guinness Stout. She headed for the self-checkout line. Undaunted she tapped the "start shopping" icon, located the bar code, slid it across the infra-red beam, and smacked the "pay now" button. She had made it through the check-out lane and back to the trike in record time.

Using two bungee cords, she secured the six-pack behind her seat in the basket. She hit the kick-start with authority and continued to ride on the sidewalk back to Mike's Market, where her groceries were waiting in the cold box.

Kat waltzed into the store and saw Mike behind the register.

"I'm back for my groceries, and I have my beer," Kat said joyfully. "Oh, and by the way, I found a quick way to get to that store, you just—"

Amused, Mike cut her off. "I would rather have my kidney removed with a grapefruit spoon than follow your suggestion on that, Kat." Then pointing, he added, "They're behind the cottage cheese and half and half in the cold box."

"Well then, never mind. I am off for Manhattans with Denney. I found my stuff. Thanks again for watching my groceries... later!"

Promptly at six p.m., Kat appeared on the spacious patio Denney had designed. The warm brie, water crackers, and grapes were already tastefully arranged on Mother's china on the patio table.

Kat sank into the hammock and stretched out. Denney took the groceries into the kitchen, put them away and came back to the porch with a pitcher of their favorite, amber-colored refreshment.

"Here it is, my own recipe," said Denney, closing the French doors behind her. She placed the pitcher on the table and reached for the old-fashioned glasses. Denney's Manhattans were not the ones currently in vogue at most bars. Hers was far and away smoother and more rejuvenating. Closer, she maintained, to the original recipe created for the scion of the Rockefeller family some generations back.

She poured the amber elixir for Kat and herself. Then she removed a cushion from a chair and sat down. "The cushions feel too hot to me just now," she said. Turning to Kat, she inquired, "Do you have the post office pick-up with you?"

Kat was asleep.

Denney was more than perturbed; she was agitated. All that preparation and her sister dared to doze off. Quietly, she slipped over to the hammock and pulled down on its side, tossing Kat out.

"My God, Denney, what happened?"

"Just one of those strong night breezes, I suspect," Denney cooed.

"By the way, Kat, what did you pick up from the post office?"

"Let me get it." She pulled herself up slowly and hobbled inside to retrieve the envelope from her suitcase. She became panicky as she could only remember getting it but not where it ended up. Chagrinned, she walked back to the patio to give Denney the bad news. To her amazement, she found her to be forgiving about the whole thing.

"Not to worry. Was there anything peculiar or memorable about the envelope?" Denney asked.

"I noticed the postage. It was mailed from here in New Orleans. Otherwise, there was no return address, and our names were typed on a standard mailing label. It had several forwarding stamps from the Post Office and looked like it had made the rounds of houses before it was delivered to us. It did look like it was done on a very old standard typewriter with a bad ribbon. You know, the kind of ribbon that pulled a little of the red ink from the bottom with each key stroke. Overall, it was a mess."

Denney had found her mint candy while rummaging in her handbag during Kat's description of the outside of the envelope. She gingerly peeled off the wrapper and popped it into her mouth.

Kat exclaimed, "Oh, one other thing. Mrs. Merriweather told me Ashleigh has a twin brother. That's all, just that he has a brother. Evidently, the Colonel told her years ago there were two Daggit boys. The whereabouts of Ashleigh's brother is unknown."

"I don't remember. When we moved away, all those earlier contacts were lost to me," added Denney.

"I don't remember either. The only recollection I have of the Daggits is of Ashleigh, and that is only as an adult."

***

Denney took the small piece of plastic wrap and deposited the remainder of the piece of candy in the wrapper saying softly to herself, "I'll just save this for later." She then pursed her lips and said, "Now we have something to think about and more if we can verify Merriweather's disclosure. You know she drinks way too much."

They were tired from their day and started to retreat to their bedrooms when they saw flashing lights approach. A police cruiser pulled up to the curb in front of their house. The officer rolled down his window and called to them, "Ladies, you wouldn't have happened to see anyone on a trike riding down the sidewalks as if he or maybe she thought it was their own personal driveway?"

Denney just shrugged and turned to Kat. She adopted a thoughtful and serious expression and said, "No, officer. Sorry. Have a good night." Denney held the door open for Kat so they could both leave the porch together. Once inside, Denney said, "Kat, that was *you*."

I'll take the Mark V to drive for a while, at least until the heat is off," Kat replied, while puzzling over the officer's comment "*he* or maybe she." Kat was relieved she had arranged for the car to be brought to New Orleans so it would be ready for them to use for their stay.

Chapter 11

Look for Ballast

Winston sat in his travel camper. He bought it from a guy who had it stashed on his property in a weedy back lot. No attempt at trying to keep it clean was evident. Drab and discolored, it rested on at least one flat tire that he could see through the overgrown weeds. As he forked over $3000.00, he thought other than a round balloon, few things looked as non-aerodynamic as this rusted-out piece of shit. Once he parked it in a trashed-out trailer park and paid a month's lot rent, he poured himself four fingers of bourbon and leaned back in a ratty recliner jammed inside the interior of the camper. Earlier, he had listened to the sister's conversation on an illegal wiretap as Denney made reservations to play golf. Agitated, he thought that should be him, hobnobbing with other club members, swinging a golf club, and sending a ball in flight. He quickly poured himself another healthy shot and plotted against them in earnest.

***

Denney had made an early tee time for nine holes of golf. She had decided it would be good for them to take their mind off the current perplexing problems and enjoy the outdoors.

"Obviously, we need to start with the Bypass Store and Auction. We already know Beau Buford, and we know the Colonel had dealings with him as well," said Denney.

"Is it open today?" inquired Kat.

"No, not 'til tomorrow."

"Great," Kat said enthusiastically. "We can play golf now before heading out tomorrow for Buford's."

***

Denney called to Kat from the kitchen, "An early start is the only way to beat the heat and stay fresh for the rest of the afternoon, Kat." She impatiently tapped her foot on the kitchen floor.

"Okay, Okay, I'm coming, Denney. While I brush my teeth, tell me about this course you found."

Calling up the stairs, she said, "I must say, I amaze myself on this fine choice of a course. It looks for easy play, and it has no water features, nice straight fairways, not an abundance of sand traps, LOTS of shade, and the golf carts have little electric fans to help keep me cool. OH YES, they have a CART GIRL who will bring us drinks other than soda."

As Kat walked into the kitchen, she asked Denney, "Are you sure you didn't just book us nine holes in someone's front yard?"

"I may not know golf courses as well as you, Kat, but I assure you this is a nice course, a reasonably priced course at that," scolded Denney. "I can't offhand remember the name, but no matter, I have the GPS coordinates on my phone."

As Kat stood at the kitchen counter with her latte, Denney twirled around in her golf skirt and matching collared shirt. "What do you think?"

"Not bad sis, I like the color on you. The pale yellow with trim in gray... nice. The shoes are divine—with the vintage scrollwork on the toes and the off-white color, all that *vintage*. I may have to borrow those!" Denney may have picked up some weight over the years, but she still had nice legs.

"Thank you." Denney was delighted. "I'm ready to go. When are you going to be ready?"

Kat was wearing cargo shorts with a Stinky's Seafood t-shirt. "I thought I was ready."

"Fine," said Denney. "If anyone asks, you're my caddy."

"Denney, you raise the garage door and I'll lock the back door."

The Mark V had plenty of room for two golf bags and a double bed if necessary. Kat stowed their bags and slid into the passenger side of the front seat.

Denney, on occasion, would drive them to their destination. She preferred not to drive at all but be driven everywhere because she did not feel safe in smaller models like Kat's Vespa. She never drove home from anywhere. Kat was the designated driver on the way home, as they were usually a little squiffy from their many daily cocktails. Denney insisted Kat drive as she could defend her on charges but not herself. Having a law degree had its advantages.

But today, Denney drove down the highway following complicated directions spoken to her by an Australian male voice on her GPS app. Kat apprehensively kept an eye on the fuel gauge as the Mark V was the least fuel-efficient car ever made.

Denney pulled up, reaching the course with a quarter of a tank to spare. She parked the car under some shade provided by a towering live oak. She sighed contentedly as she felt all was going according to plan, and she was pleased with herself. They retrieved their clubs from the trunk and looked around for the clubhouse or the starter's box. She pointed to a small cabana-type shelter about half a mile away.

"Maybe that's where we're supposed to go," said Kat.

Puzzled at this turn of events, Denney responded, "It may not be the caliber of play at Harbor Town at Sea Pines, but we've been banned from those kinds of courses, anyway."

"No kidding," said Kat. "After you continually parked the cart on the greens because your shoes were a little too snug. You refused to walk. We would have to wear disguises to get in any real nice golf course and have fake IDs as well since they made a copy of ours and distributed our pictures just about everywhere."

"You exaggerate. But I think the fake ID might work!"

Denney shielded her eyes and gazed towards the cabana. "Are you telling me we have to walk there with our clubs?" She already had lip perspiration beginning, and her mood was turning sour.

"We could drive," suggested Kat.

"There's no road." Denney shielded her eyes. "All I see is just a weedy lot to traverse."

Kat was becoming impatient. "Do you want to play golf or not? It's bound to get better."

Denney pulled out her club carrier with wheels and strapped her clubs in. She noticed that Kat did not have a carrier. Kat pulled out a five wood, seven iron, pitching wedge, and putter and placed them in Denney's bag. There were balls in both pockets with tees and a glove. Kat left her bag in the trunk, turned to Denney and said, "Okay, let's go."

They were glistening with sweat when they finally reached the cabana. Their socks were covered with sticky milkweed, the Velcro of weeds.

"Where's the course and the cart girl? Where is anyone for that matter?" Denney asked while pulling her damp clothes away from her body.

Kat was fanning herself with her ball cap and looking around for anyone who could help them.

"My God, it's hot," said Denney. "I'm parched."

The small shelter that housed the carts and refreshment counter seemed devoid of employees. As Kat rounded the corner to grab something to drink, the cabana boy strode into sight with a wonderfully cool concoction in his hand. He studied the two women.

Denney immediately called out her demands. "Young man, we would like to play some golf. We have a tee time, you know, and would you please set me up with whatever you're having."

Denney grimaced but signed the registration book, a spiral notebook one sees in high school for taking class notes, with her customary flourish. "Now, don't be skimpy on whatever you're putting in that drink. Oh yes and fix one of those for my caddy as well. I am quite thirsty, and a little something extra would help calm the nerves."

The cabana boy tapped Kat on the shoulder and handed her the score cards, which looked as if they had already been used once due to the eraser marks and tossed her a cart key as well. He winked at her and told her he would make hers "extra strong."

Denney tipped the cabana boy, and they made their way to the cart. By the time they had their clubs secured and the small fans set on high, the cabana boy returned with their drinks. Kat turned on the battery-powered cart and sped off as he watched them from a safe distance.

"Wow, I don't know what this is, but it's spectacular, I can tell you that," said Kat.

Denney took a long sip from her drink. She agreed and, raising her glass outside the cart, shouted over her shoulder, "Attendant, bring us two more on the fifth hole, will you?"

Denney usually chose what she thought were the correct clubs for their first drive of the day, another ritual. She chose Big Bertha for herself. She was into power. She was dismayed the only option for Kat was the five wood. Kat was okay with that, proclaiming she was the queen of the five wood. Neither sister kept score. The score card was used to record how many drinks they consumed. As they sped on to the next hole, they were enjoying themselves and were happy with their progress so far.

When they reached the fifth hole, ready for a refill, Denney anxiously looked around for the drink cart. "Kat, do you see the young man with our round of refreshments anywhere?"

"I think he's coming over that rise as you speak."

The cabana boy pulled up and hopped off his cart. He brought over two extra-tall glasses of his specialty, and Denney tipped him generously, and he quickly bounced off.

Kat took a long swallow of her drink while scanning the sky behind them. "It looks a little gray over there, don't you think?"

Denney looked up and behind her and then turned and looked in front of her. "It's behind us, Kat, not to worry. Smooth sailing up front," she pronounced. Ever since she completed her "Junior Sailor" course in the Bahamas, she considered herself a weather expert.

The sisters were motoring toward the eighth hole, enjoying their refreshments, and knuckle bumping on the green.

"This is great fun." Denney giggled. "We needed this outing!"

"I can't believe how well we're playing," replied Kat.

As the sisters pulled up to the tee box on the eighth hole, the heavens decided to open for a monster popup storm.

"Jesus, Joseph, and Mary!" shouted Denney as a sharp crack of lightning exploded near enough to make the hair on her arms stand at attention.

Kat dropped her drink and took off at a dead run for the cart. Denney was fast on her heels.

Kat was getting a little panicky. "What should we do?"

"Get in and hold fast!" directed Denney just before she stomped on the cart's gas pedal and took off.

Denney had a shocked faraway look in her eyes. "Hoist the main mast and catch the wind, sailor! I fear we are in a storm-tossed ship."

Kat looked worriedly at Denney as she sped across fairways and greens, churning up what little bent grass the course had while racing through the rain to try to reach the car. The rain was coming down so hard the golf cart was taking on water anywhere it could settle. The cup holders, the front compartment, the cooler, and sandbox—all were overflowing.

Denney looked at the collecting water and screamed over the claps of thunder, "Ballast, ballast, we need ballast in the bilge for a stable float in this schooner!"

"Okay, Denney, I'll look for ballast." Kat started pulling everything she could find out of the golf bag and started stuffing it into crevices and compartments in the golf cart.

As they rounded the ninth hole, they were at the turn, and Denney spied the cabana and roared, "Port ahead!"

"Just pass up that spit of land and go for the yacht. Do you see it over there anchored safely in the cove? We can board and stow our gear," Kat eagerly suggested.

Denney sharply turned toward the direction of their car. She stomped on the gas pedal and sent milkweed flying as she sped over the field between the course and the car. Stopping short of careening into the passenger side, she vaulted out of the golf cart and into the front passenger seat.

Kat stowed the clubs in the monstrous cavity of the Mark V called a trunk and left the ballast in the cart. Chap Stick, bug spray, extra socks, lipstick, Band-Aids, all were floating in the water and left behind.

Though soggy and out of breath, Kat hopped into the front seat behind the wheel and asked casually, "How about lunch?"

Denney seemed to be more herself now as the wipers slapped soothingly back and forth on the windshield of the Mark V. She positioned the rearview mirror so she could look at herself. She was taken aback at her now frizzy and visor-shaped hair.

"Oh crap, I can't enjoy eating anything looking like this!" she moaned. She was in no mood to be seen in public.

As much as she would like to have an artisan chopped salad, she would never risk exposing herself to the sort of criticism reserved for older women who didn't give a damn about how they looked.

"Just let me do something with my hair before we go," said Denney.

Kat thought there was more repair work to be done than just hair but was relieved Denney was more herself and was hungry.

Chapter 12

NASA Cap and Caramels

Once they reached the house, they kicked off their grass-covered golf shoes and headed for their rooms. Denney grabbed the blow dryer and straightened her hair as best she could and changed from her golf clothes into silky yoga pants and top. She grabbed her sandals and made her way downstairs, where she saw Kat was already pacing.

Kat had pulled her hair back, grabbed another ball cap—her favorite with the NASA logo on the front. She had started wearing it more often after she and Denney were in the check-out line at Walmart, and the cashier asked Kat if she worked at NASA. Kat seamlessly lied about being a rocket scientist but was currently retired. The look of impressed envy on the face of the woman scanning her purchases was divine. Denney was appalled.

"Denney, are you gonna wear those silk yoga pants to go out to lunch?" Kat started to sit down on one of the stools at the kitchen island, it tipped, and she slid off, catching herself before she fell on the floor. In doing so, she reinjured her hip. The old dirt bike injury was surely aggravated, and the pain was immediate.

Denney was exasperated and asked, "Can you move at all? Because it's getting late and Dr. Whoolery, my chiropractor, closes at three p.m. today."

Kat winced as she tried to move from her bent position.

"That settles it! We need to get you in the car and seen by someone now," Denney said.

Denney took Kat's arm and tried to help her stand up straight. It was a pitiful sight. Kat had to contort herself to find a position where she could stand. Then there was the walk. The green and gold Moravian carpet runner looked like the long green mile.

She remembered that Kat liked the Colonel's walking sticks and had over time collected a few. They were in the umbrella stand. Denney fetched one. Kat was doing her best to hobble down the hall to the front door when she grabbed the cane from Denney. "Now to get down the steps to the sidewalk," coached Denney. "Kat, how will you ever get down those steps?"

They both stopped in their tracks. It looked impossible.

Kat blinked a couple of times and stared down at the steps. She pulled her cell phone from her back pocket and dialed 911. Screaming into the phone, "Help, help, I've fallen, and I can't get up." She thought she sounded just like the commercial and was pleased with the effort, which quickly affected a solution to the problem. She mused that maybe she could have been a rocket scientist after all. She propped herself up against the column of the porch and waited with anticipation while EMS triangulated the call. She had left the location engaged on her phone and was hopeful.

Denney was mortified. The only possible solution was a small glass of sherry, which she poured into a fine diamond-cut two-ounce liqueur glass. While she was in the solitude of the den, never mentioning to share with Kat lest the medics think she was an old sot rather than the rocket scientist she was going to feign to be. Denney knew her sister well.

"Denney, I know what you're doing in there! Good grief, I think they sent the whole fire department here. I can see them coming, and you're gonna miss their arrival if you don't get out here." The fire truck was rounding the corner, but still no Denney. As they bounded up the porch, stretcher in tow, Denney came out holding her glass of sherry.

"What? A stretcher? Isn't that a bit overdone? Just hoist her up under the armpits and set her down," said Denney.

The two EMTs looked at Denney as if she was surely kidding. She wasn't. Of the two men, the older one was more attractive, she thought. The younger one was too thin, but he did seem strong enough to maneuver Kat onto the stretcher and into the ambulance. She started to make her way to the ambulance to ride along when the younger EMT stopped her.

"Excuse me, ma'am, but you can't ride along. We will take good care of your yard man, uh, person, and you can inquire later."

"I beg your pardon, young man. She is certainly NOT a caretaker for my property," Denney said angrily. "*SHE* is a scientist, a rocket scientist no less, and you should know that as she is *wearing* her ball cap! We live in this house together!"

The older EMT winked at the younger one and said something under his breath about being "politically correct" while taking Denney's hand and helping her into the back of the ambulance. Denney allowed how family members are more often told to follow while partners can ride along.

"No one wants a possible scene upon arrival," Denney said knowingly to Kat.

Kat knocked a few rolls of gauze and tape off a nearby shiny aluminum tray and tried to see herself in the muddy reflection.

"He wasn't sure of my gender!" she gasped as she pulled her knees to her chest and rocked back and forth to calm herself. Kat was grateful that Denney had joined her in the back of the ambulance. If nothing else, she could clarify some of the mystery surrounding her gender.

Denney saw Kat rocking with a wild-eyed look. Denney smirked and told Kat that it appeared she had recovered. "What you gonna do now, Spike?"

"Stop it, Denney, people are starting to think I'm a guy! This sucks!"

Denney laughed. "Well, if you didn't wear those

hideous black trainers, they might think otherwise."

"Well, maybe all I need is a padded bra."

"No, then they'd just think you were trans."

The EMT was ready to lower Kat's gurney to the ground and rush her to the ER by the time the ride ended.

Kat looked worriedly at Denney and asked, "How are we going to get—"

Denney put her finger to her lips and shushed Kat, "We'll UBER it home."

Upon reaching the hospital ER, Kat put her hand to her neck and searched frantically. "Denney, I don't have my amulet or my cross. If I'm gonna go inside there, I need one of 'em," she said in a distraught whisper. "Can you go back to the house and get one? You know where they are, right? Next to the bottle of Pepto on the bedside table."

"I'll go home and bring back your cross. Forget the amulet. If I came back to Advent Hospital with that, I'd feel like a hippo in a carp pond. My buzz has worn off anyway."

Denney left the ER waiting room and sauntered over to the hospital gift shop, thinking a quick trip to stop, and shop might be fun. She always liked to look at the cards and kept a few handy for unexpected events. As she walked into the gift shop, she saw Winky Danville, a fellow St. Kitt's member and a candy-making rival at the candy counter.

Winky loved to talk about her membership at an expensive spa, when she was an avid, ordinary gym rat in reality. Her tall, thin body was reasonably defined. Her hair was naturally gray but always, *always* styled. Denney realized that Winky competed on a slightly less-than-conscious level with everyone but particularly with her.

Winky had married well and had all the creature comforts. Unlike herself, Winky was moderate in her drinking habits, but Denney knew she was sought after and garnered much more than her fair share of attention, and she knew Winky knew it too. Furthermore, Denney was her arch enemy when it came to candy. Denney preferred hard candy with a tart and sweet component, while her rival, Winky, always made gooey soft candy.

This rivalry continued throughout the year but hit its zenith around Christmas when Winky would make her chocolate Goo Goo's and Denney would make her kumquat hard candy for the church Christmas bazaar.

Some years Winky's would sell more, and some years Denney's would sell more. It was constant combat. But being arch enemies ensured they would always be extremely civil, yet crafty, to one another.

"Whatever brings you *here*, all the way from Louisville, Winky?" cooed Denney.

"Oh, Lyndeeeen, my niece just had a baby, and I came to visit," Winky replied sweetly in her exaggerated Southern voice. Winky was always formal when addressing Denney, and she never pronounced her name correctly.

"Oh really, I'll have to send her a card." She smirked as she chose a sympathy card with a bowl of sugar-coated lemon drops on the front. "This will do just fine," she exclaimed.

Taking the opportunity to zing Winky a couple of more times, Denney continued, "By the way, if you're leaving, would you mind ever so much to drop me off at the house? I came here with Kat in an ambulance and needed to pick up a few things for her at home and bring them back."

Winky knew it would be bad manners to decline, and she was curious to know what happened. She would never ignore potentially good gossip. "Oh, bless her heart! Of course, Lindeeeen. I would be glad to provide you with any help you need. Now, what happened to poor Kathay?"

"Oh, it's her hip or sciatica. Poor thing, she couldn't move at all." Denney was watching Winky's every move to see what she was reaching for.

As Winky edged over to the soft candy display, she sympathized. "You know I get that too! Flares up now and then. I hope this doesn't mean you'll miss our dinner tonight."

Denney was rarely caught off guard, but she could not remember an invitation, let alone a confirmation for dinner with Winky. While she racked her brain for a memory, Winky took advantage and grabbed a bag of soft caramel candy, telling the girl at the register to send it immediately to Kat's room or the ER, whichever place she was now.

Denney turned to Winky, received the forfeit, and announced, "To the car, Winky, I don't have time to fritter away." As Winky headed to the car looking smug, Denney purchased a bag of hard candy to "share" on the way home.

***

Upstairs Kat was enjoying all the attention a rocket scientist deserves. They even provided her with a private room in the VIP wing. She kept the channel turned to the science programs so she could make pithy remarks now and again. She was informed she would be staying the night with discharge tomorrow. She sent one of the candy stripers to buy her a nice pair of PJs and to send up a huge spray of flowers for the room. She intended to sign the card "from all your friends at NASA."

Since she was not on a restricted diet, she ordered delivery of a gourmet pizza for dinner. As she patiently waited for all her stuff to arrive, she left a message on the house phone for Denney that she would be discharged tomorrow a.m. and to come and see her around dinner time as she had ordered out for food delivery, adding that Denney could slip the Manhattan mix in her shoulder bag. While she waited for the answering machine to pick up, she reached into a candy bowl and grabbed a couple of just-arrived caramels.

Chapter 13

Lindene, You Can Sure Be a Bitch

Early in the morning, Denney called Kat, and they decided a cab could bring her home, and Denney would have freshly brewed coffee and biscotti ready.

Kat returned home feeling much better. She had a new prescription for pain medicine and felt well enough to check out Beau Buford's Bypass Store and Auction with Denney.

Denney decided she would drive the Mark V to the furniture store and see if Kat was well enough to drive home. She hated driving but acquiesced in times of need. As she pulled up in front of the store, she took up two parking places, parking at an angle. She slid out of the car and walked around to the passenger side to see if Kat needed any assistance.

"No, I'm okay, really," Kat said reassuringly as she rattled her pill bottle.

They entered the store. Denney spoke with the proprietor, Beau, a ne'er do well. Kat looked around and came closer to where Denney was talking with Mr. Buford and tried to appear as if she wasn't listening.

"Do you recall selling or auctioning a desk that may have belonged to the Colonel?" asked Denney.

"Do you have some sort of ID?" he said peevishly, although he knew perfectly well who she was. "You need to tell me more about it before I start looking."

"Why Beau Buford, you know I wouldn't ask for a copy of documents if it wasn't legally necessary!"

Beau shot back, "Everything is legally necessary with you, Lindene."

"What kind of slur is that?" said Denney.

"Well, you know, you're always throwing around your education, and that makes folks feel bad," Beau complained.

"I am only looking for verification you auctioned off a desk for the Colonel's benefit and who the buyer was. The Colonel passed away about six months ago, and this was a purchase within a year or so of his death. That should narrow it down. How many auctions do you do in a year, anyway?"

Beau had plopped himself down in his chair behind his desk. With his hands resting on his substantial belly, he yawned and creaked back in his chair till he perched on the back legs.

"I do a lot more business, including auctions, than you think."

Unfazed by this announcement, she said, "Oh really? Well, I was just making a point."

Beau leveled his chair, his elbows and forearms planted on the desktop. He was glaring at Denney. "I'm not gonna go into the attic and search through old dusty boxes for some old inventory list from an auction when I don't have a start date," he shouted.

Denney placed her hands on her hips, looked over the rim of her Diane von Furstenberg sunglasses, and said, "well… you… are… going… to… have… to… do… it … anyway."

Beau, thoroughly exasperated by now, became even more stubborn and leaned over his desk with beads of sweat popping out along his brow. "Make me," he said calmly but with a fair amount of churlishness.

Kat stopped looking around the store and perched herself on a dining room table to watch. She knew Beau could not win this contest, but he was giving it a good try. Denney was about to change tactics.

Denney paced in front of Beau's desk with a calm, thoughtful look on her face. Kat knew how dangerous this new tactic was even though Beau did not.

"Think of it as a way to purge some of your old papers, you know… the ones the IRS might find interesting." She paused in front of his desk and waited.

"I pay my taxes!" Beau blurted out defensively.

"You may pay yours, but what about all those housekeepers you had before Edna said she would marry you just to stop you from stalking her? I think you referred to them as some of your visiting cousins?" questioned

Denney.

Kat quietly announced, "Score!" She hopped off the table to look around the store once again.

Beau, in the meantime, was red in the face. He stood with both hands gripping the back of his chair. He conceded defeat but not gracefully as he spoke. "Lindene, you can sure be a bitch."

"I try to be the best at everything I do, Beau."

Beau, exhausted from his parlay with her announced tiredly, "Give me a few days. It's hot and dusty in the attic, and I'll have to wait till it cools off some in the evening. All that dust, and for what? I can barely breathe up there, and it probably won't amount to anything. I used to store my stash up there, and I don't want Edna to even think I'm into that again. She would surely kill me this time."

Denney looked for Kat and tossed over her shoulder, "I'm sure she won't even notice your absence."

Kat had found an old Darth Vader mask with a working respirator rigged into the mask itself, and she set it on Beau's desk.

"You think that is going to help?" Denny asked Kat.

They returned home. Kat was able to drive, much to Denney's relief.

***

They made their way out to the front porch to discuss the events of the day. They came to no definite conclusion but felt they were headed in the right direction to get some answers.

It was dark now, so they cleaned up their dishes and made their way upstairs. Both commented on how they missed their dogs. They would have been slumbering beside them at night. They decided they wanted to wrap up business here as soon as possible to return to their beloved animals at St. James.

***

Beau Buford was locking the store for the evening when the phone rang. The harsh ringer jarred Beau as he walked to answer it through the silent, empty store. Startled, he picked up the receiver at the end of the second ring. Before he could answer, a deep, threatening male voice said, "Buford, is that you?"

"Yeah," he answered nervously, "Who's this?

"It's Winfield, you idiot. Why did those sisters come to see you?"

Beau was wary. "How did you know that?"

"That's none of your concern. What is your concern— is to tell me why they were there. We made a deal, Buford; you tell me what I need to know when I need it, and I keep quiet about our relationship," shot back Winfield.

Beau immediately felt the pressure of this threat. Back when his store had been known as Buford's Collectibles, Beau had fenced loose stones from jewelry for Winfield. They both did well from the operation, but it abruptly stopped when Winfield was sent to prison. He knew Winfield wouldn't think twice about implicating Beau if it was to his advantage.

"They came here looking for information about a piece of furniture I sold here at auction."

"Did that involve the Colonel?"

Beau hesitated slightly with this reply. "They just want me to look for an auction bill of sale for a piece of furniture."

Winfield tersely ended the conversation. "I'll call you again to see what you turn up."

Chapter 14

It's Dark as a Cave in Here

Up early the next day, Denney and Kat were having beignets and coffee at Cafe Du Monde. While sitting outside, Denney saw a man she believed to be Ashleigh across the street.

Sipping her coffee and licking the sweet sugar off her fingers, she leaned over and whispered to Kat, "Look across the street and tell me if that is not Ashleigh."

"It sure looks like him, but that guy is dressed much more stylishly than Ashleigh ever has."

"Yeah, look at those Salvatore Ferragamo shoes! I could spot them anywhere! Whoever he is, he seems to be off to the Canal Street Ferry. If it is Ashleigh, why would *he* be *here*? He *has* been acting very curiously. I think we should follow him," said Denney. "Let's dust the sugar off and finish our coffee. You flag the waiter, and I'll walk outside to watch where the mystery man is headed."

They moved quietly and stealthily behind buildings and corners following their prey. As they reached the docked ferry, the Ashleigh lookalike headed for the upper deck. Kat decided they both should remain on the lower deck out of sight. As the ferry made its way across the Mississippi to the west bank, known as Algiers, Denney opened her handbag and pulled out a powdery beignet wrapped in a napkin.

"Seriously? Put that away. You can't possibly be that hungry," said Kat. "You need to focus. I can't have you slipping into a sugar coma."

Denney rewrapped her beignet and slipped it back into her handbag but not before she curtly replied, "You're just being ugly because you didn't bring one for yourself. Besides, I don't have any candy in my pockets in case I have to do some hard thinking."

As the ferry headed across the Mississippi for Algiers, they sat in silence. They continued to watch the stairs to make sure they would catch the lookalike if he came down. After a bit, both were about to nod off when the ferry made a rough docking and jarred them back into awareness.

"My goodness," Denney shrieked, "that just about knocked me off the bench!"

"Yep," Kat replied, "damn good thing because the Ashleigh lookalike is getting off right now. We need to hurry so as not to lose him. Step it up, Denney, let's go!"

They hustled to the exit as they watched him walk gingerly down the street.

"Where do you think he's going?" said Denney. "He seems to have a purpose to his steps. Do you know anything about Algiers and why he may be here?"

"Well, I don't know much, only that we don't want to

be here after dark; more murder happens here in the old section than in other parts of town," replied Kat. "Other than it being a historic district, there's not much going on there."

"Oh my God, Kat, let's get this over with as soon as possible, shall we? Do you know how to avoid the old part?"

"I'm all for getting it over with," added Kat, "because I don't know my way around here. Okay, he seems to be going into that bar across the way."

"Well, let's follow him and see if we can find out what in the world *he* is doing *here*."

Denney and Kat waited outside the bar and peered into the window to see how crowded it was so maybe they could blend in. The windows were grimy on the outside, so visibility was low. As more people entered the bar, Denney decided it would be safe for them to go inside.

"Kat, you go first. You look like you belong here."

"You want to explain that remark," she said crisply.

"Well, it's just that… look at you, jeans and a drab long-sleeve shirt. You look like a longshoreman. I am certainly more stylish, you must admit. My shoes alone scream good taste."

Kat slung open the door with Denney close on her heels, holding on to the back of her shirttail. They did not see him anywhere.

"Do you think he went to the can?" asked Kat.

"Well, how would I know that?" Denney pushed Kat farther into the bar.

"It's dark as a cave in here. We need to find a place in a corner and sit and wait,' said Denney. "He's got to be here somewhere." Looking around quickly, she continued, "Maybe one of those booths would suit our purposes."

Kat spied a shabby booth in the corner and pulled Denney by the hand over to it, and they sat side by side, their backs to the front window.

Denney was uncomfortable. "God, these seats are sticky. I hope nothing gets on the back of my pants. This kind of grime has to be difficult to clean." She watched Kat pull her ball cap lower over her eyes as she took in the room. She pulled some Kleenex out of her handbag so that she could slip it under her bottom to avoid stains. The barmaid stood at the end of the bar. Pencil and pad in hand, she made her way to the girls to take their order.

Denney gave the barmaid the once over and whispered to Kat, "Can you order us something and make sure you tell her to hand wash the glasses before bringing them out?"

Kat raised the bill of her ball cap and looked at the waitress, who tapped her pencil on her order pad and glared at Denney.

"Ummm, hello, would it be possible to get two Manhattans brought to our table?" Kat asked with her hands in a prayer position.

The waitress slipped the pad into the front pocket of her jeans and stared at Denney trying to position her

Kleenex just so, and said, "I think you're gonna need a couple each."

Kat glanced at Denney and said, "Oh, don't worry about her. After a couple of drinks, she's actually tolerable."

***

Unseen by the sisters, the lookalike had gone to the rear of the bar and the men's restroom. He was in deep conversation with a dirty-looking vagrant, Asmond, who had been his cellmate several years ago.

"Winfield, you're looking pretty sharp these days," Asmond said with sarcastic envy.

Dismissing Asmond's remark, Winfield scowled, "I intend to look even better when I secure my rightful inheritance. My brother Ashleigh already has money, and I can assure you I will too, in the near future. No one will stop me."

Winfield passed Asmond several folded bills. "I see our plan worked to get you out of prison. Lay low with this cash for a while. He also handed him a pre-paid phone and said, "Don't use this until you get to Louisville in a couple of weeks." He turned sharply. "Clear out now!"

Grimacing, Asmond quickly exited the bar by the back door. He did not look back as he counted the bills given him.

Winfield took one last swallow from his drink and left the bar from the rear exit, unseen by Kat or Denney.

Kat and Denney were preoccupied with a large, male,

greasy, and very muscular orange tabby steadily making its way over to their table.

"Well," said Kat, "what can we do for you, little kitty?"

The tabby purred with a low rumble and jumped up on the table next to Denney, looked out the window for a few seconds, and turned around to spray the glass with a copious amount of extraordinarily strong urine.

"What the crap?" said Denney. Enraged, she tried to brush the cat off the table, which enraged the feline. As the cat backed up with bristles raised on its neck, ears laid back, and menace in its hiss, she became alarmed. "Do something," Denney pleaded as she frantically waved a Kleenex in front of the cat's swiping paw.

Kat turned and looked at the tabby, who had now shredded the tissue and was ready to pounce. She took off her ball cap and swung with a wide arc. She knocked the cat off balance. It scrabbled to regain its grip on the edge of the table, howling like mad.

"You got it on the run now," Denney said with glee as she swiftly clocked the cat with a saltshaker. Recovering its composure, the big tabby began grooming itself near the bar. The barmaid reappeared from behind the bar with four Manhattans on a serving tray. She balanced the tray in one hand as she bent down and picked up the cat by the scruff of its neck, and deposited him on top of the bar. She gave it a quick pat, and the cat settled down, stretching its full length along the bar, carefully watching the sisters in their booth.

Denney smiled weakly at the barmaid and said, "Well dear, you're here just in time. We were trying to pet your cat, but he lost his balance and fell, poor kitty. Thank you, though for the drinks. You are very prompt, I must say— and wow, it's happy hour. One would hope you remembered to wash the glasses before you made us our luscious drinks. Ehh?"

Kat took the drinks and chugged the first one down. Denney sipped her first drink and tried not to notice the cat urine that dripped down the glass behind her. As she looked around the bar, which was beginning to fill with seedy patrons, she signaled the barmaid to bring two more rounds of drinks for each of them.

Denney puckered her mouth and said, "These Manhattans are deplorable, but they are strong, a saving grace and all that." She had finished off her first drink and was almost finished with the second.

"Yeah, and I intend to have plenty of them. That cat urine is atomic grade, and I hope I won't notice it pretty soon."

"Really? I must have a slight sinus problem," slurred Denney.

They matched each other drink for drink.

Denney, now relaxed, slung her arm on the backrest of the booth precariously close to the urine-drenched window. She tapped her manicured nails on the duct-taped top of the booth back. Deep in thought, she pulled out a tissue she had been sitting on to dab her mouth.

Kat now had her ball cap on backward and forgot to care about being recognized. "Denney, let's order two more and then I'll swing back towards the restrooms and take a peek. We haven't seen our 'unsub' since we've been here."

Denney noticed that Kat again slipped into her detective jargon from her noir crime novels.

The girls polished off their fifth Manhattan each. Daylight no longer existed, and the night was inky black. Patrons were beginning to leave the bar as Kat tried to get up to go to the restrooms located in the back to check on the Ashleigh lookalike.

"Golly, Denney, I don't think I can make it to the bathrooms. Can you go and check it out?"

Denney could get out of the booth but had to hold on to chair backs to steady herself as she tried to make her way to the back of the bar. She was almost there when she saw the orange tabby lounging by the restroom doors. The cat stretched out while lying down and exposed one paw with claws unsheathed while looking at her through one slanted open eye. She turned around and made her way back to the booth where Kat was slumped, with her head down on the table, snoring lightly.

"Wake up, Kat, there is no Ashleigh. We need to leave," she said, "and make our way back to the house to rest for tomorrow."

Kat slid out from behind the booth, saluted the cat, and held Denney's arm as they left the bar. "Which way do we go? I seem to be a little foggy on directions right now."

Denney helped Kat make their way slowly to the dock but read on the posted sign that the last ferry left at eight p.m. That was hours ago. Also, the bridge was closed—only for emergency use this evening—no cars in and no cars out till six a.m.

"Damn," said Denney. We must find a place to sleep and a restroom. Pull out your cell and google us up something."

Kat checked her pockets but had no phone. "I don't have my cell," she said as she leaned against the railing of the dock.

"Well, where is it?" Denney asked icily.

"Beats the hell out of me," said Kat, burping.

Now exasperated with their situation, Denney said, "I guess I will have to use mine. This is so typical. I have to save the situation once again." She searched her purse and tossed items on the pavement, looking for her phone. No phone.

Denney looked at Kat and stared out in space. "What are we going to do now?"

Kat realized the situation could become dire and answered, "We should look for a gas station for a restroom and maybe a church; it looks like rain. Maybe something Catholic as they might have a late mass, and we could implore someone to take us in until the morning or just even sleep on a pew."

"Okay, Denney said brightly, her mood changing abruptly. "Let's walk up and down those streets over there.

I have a feeling about them. Catholic churches are overstated architecturally, so some design feature, a bell perhaps, should show up over the top of the houses." Meeting the challenge, she started off. Kat stumbled along beside her while she charted a course.

"AHA," Denney shouted, "look to the right! I have found our refuge. It's perfect. We will just knock on the door of... let me see... *Holy Name of St. Peter Church,* it says, and perhaps a lone priest or sympathetic nun will still be hanging around cleaning candleholders or whatnot, and we can seek shelter inside!"

They reached the doors of the church and knocked repeatedly. No one came. Denney muttered, "How uncharitable the Catholics have become."

Kat looked at her with frustration. "How could they tell so quickly that we were Episcopalians?"

Kat spied a part of the front porch sheltered by some shrubbery. "Denney, come and sit beside me, we have done the best we can, and we will just have to wait it out. Nothing to do at this time."

"I don't have any more tissues, and I loathe sitting down on this bare concrete. I've sat in enough refuse today and put up with enough grime to last me for a lifetime." Denney found a plastic grocery bag jammed under one of the bushes and pulled it out to sit on. Then she retrieved the beignet from her purse. "Dinner?"

"Lord," said Kat, "we may be on these church steps for real, sharing scraps."

Exhausted and frustrated, Denney said, "We came to New Orleans to find our inheritance. What started as curiosity about Ashleigh having a double life, and being in Algiers now, has diverted us from our real goal, which was to find out about the desk."

"Yeah, we need to concentrate our effort on the desk."

As soon as she settled in, Kat had become very sleepy and rested her head on her sister's shoulder. She began to softly sing a favorite song of hers, "The Weight," as sung by Robbie Robertson.

As she sang, Denney dug out an old Kentucky Fried Chicken bucket from under yet another shrub and began to beat out a rhythm on the upside-down barrel. A light rain started to come down as Kat sang and she drummed. A large orange tabby took all this in from a safe distance under a thick hedge. They drifted off to sleep while the tabby inched forward one micrometer at a time.

Chapter 15

There's Feral Cat There.

The sun was just starting to come up as Kat awakened with a start and looked around. Denney was still fast asleep with now very frizzy hair. She wondered if she was going to have to give up her ball cap. She looked around and remembered their evening. Next to Denney was the Kentucky Fried Chicken barrel turned on its side with the large orange tabby curled up inside. She nudged Denney carefully so as not to awaken the cat.

Denney stretched her arms over her head, yawned, and tried to focus. "Where in the hell *are* we? I can hardly move. I'm stiff as a board. We weren't evicted from our home, were we?" She took off her reading glasses and polished them to see more clearly.

"No, be careful that you don't hit that cardboard barrel 'cause there's a feral cat in there," Kat whispered.

"Oh my God! Is that the horrible feline from the bar?" shrieked Denney. "How have we fallen so low we are on the doorstep of a church with a flea-bitten cat as our companion? I'll be devastated if anyone hears about this."

"If that's what you're worried about, then let's get

going before the staff gets here. We can get a ferry out. We don't need anyone finding us like this," said Kat.

Denney shifted her weight to her hands and knees to help her get up off the concrete. The backside of her ivory tinted pants was soiled with grime and a big wad of pink bubble gum that had partially absorbed the porch dirt of hundreds if not thousands of churchgoers' shoes. Kat decided not to make her aware of this so as not to set off another alarm.

With Denney leading, they eventually made their way to the ferry and waited in line to enter. She was mollified that they were given a wide berth and quickly moved to the front of the line. She chose a seat at the rail to help redirect the scent of cigarette smoke and stale beer wafting off their clothes.

After boarding and a quick crossing of the Mississippi, they were deposited at the foot of Canal Street.

Denney insisted they buy large hats once they disembarked, hoping not to be recognized on the way home. She believed this was possible because anyone who knew her would never have believed she would be seen in public as she looked now. She wasn't so sure about Kat. They arrived home to take long baths and throw their clothes in the trash bin. Denney howled from down the hall when she realized what her pants and hair really looked like for the first time. They both took a long nap after downing several extra-strength ibuprofen.

Denney was up first and had made fresh coffee for herself and Kat, who woke to the smell of brewed coffee and sauntered down to the kitchen.

"Good afternoon, Kat. I hope the nap helped refresh you as much as it has done for me. We still have some investigating to do today. And by the way, we left our phones here, in the kitchen. Mine was still plugged in the charger!"

"We never... well, at least you never do that. Wow, I'm still a little foggy, but coffee and something to eat should bring me around. What are you thinking?" asked Kat.

"Let's take our coffee to the back porch as it is a little more shaded there, and we can discuss my plan," said Denney.

As the sisters settled in their chairs, they sipped their coffee, enjoying the comfort they so missed the night before. Denney unwrapped a lemon drop.

"Where did you get that? Kat asked. I didn't know we had a candy bowl back here."

"We don't." Denney appeared to be deep in thought but added, "I do have pockets, you know."

"I was thinking, Kat, why don't you call Carmen to check on Ashleigh's whereabouts. She generally knows information like this as everyone confides in her. She is such a good source of knowledge."

"Sure, I can do that. After I place the call, we can get with Beau and find out what he knows."

"It sounds like we're on track again after that rather dark episode in Algiers," Denney said woefully.

"Oh, I don't know. I was beginning to think well of that cat. He did have spunk, which was admirable," she said with a touch of fondness in her voice.

"That cat!" Denney nearly shouted, "STANK!"

"Well, yes, he did." Kat smiled, got up, and went to the kitchen to use one of the extensions of the house phone to call Carmen.

She answered in her usual cheerful voice. "Hello, my dear friend, what can I do for you today? By the way, the dogs are fine," said Carmen.

"Never a doubt in my mind it would be otherwise. I was wondering if you had seen Ashleigh around this weekend, say since Friday?"

"I have. I know exactly how he has been spending his time. You will be surprised, I think, to find out. He has been a counselor at the weekend lockdown at the church for middle schoolers. Playing games, eating pizza, staying up late, you know how those things go. Anyway, he has not left the church since early Friday afternoon. Everyone says he has done a wonderful job with the middle schoolers. Such a nice thing for him, don't you think?"

"That is a surprise. Is the air conditioning working at top capacity at the church?" asked Kat.

"Oh yes, they even brought the big fans. The kids were asked to bring a sweater or maybe some light fleece if they got a little chilly, but everyone seemed to be happy other than that! Hot chocolate even in this time of year was a big hit as well."

"Wonderful news," said Kat. "Denney and I are going to be leaving New Orleans either late tonight or early tomorrow morning to come back to St. James. Will you still be able to watch the dogs for just a little while longer?"

"Not a problem. We are all doing well. Safe travels, and we will look forward to seeing you soon. Give Denney a hug!"

Kat caught Denney up to date on the conversation with Carmen and what she had shared about Ashleigh.

Denney gasped. "So, if Ashleigh was in Louisville, then who was that Ashleigh lookalike guy we followed? Oh well, here we go again. We agreed to put that aside."

"I know we did, but think about it," said Kat. "Who was that guy that looked like Ashleigh? I just can't believe some guy is lurking around, in the parade, at the funeral, and now in Algiers. Don't you think he may be important in all of this somehow?"

"Remember the conversation with Merriweather and the 'twin' issue?"

"Well, that would make sense for sure about who this is," replied Kat. "Ashleigh is in Louisville, so this concerns me."

"When we get home, we can see what we can find out."

Denney grabbed her cell and made hurried plans to return to Louisville that night so that they might catch up with Ashleigh before he was released from church on Sunday.

Having made the flight arrangements, Denney called Beau at the Bypass next. They needed to run over and check with him about what he may have found in the attic before they left.

She hated to be so rushed. "Kat, you'd better drive to Beau's. I'm just too overwrought."

"For Pete's sake, Denney?" Kat asked incredulously. She grabbed the keys off the table and headed off to the Mark V but paused to lean against the wall to steady her balance as she was still a little hungover. She hoped the coffee would kick in before she had to navigate traffic in the enormous gangster mobile.

As they drove along, Denney hummed cheerily in the passenger side, making small talk until they reached the store.

When they arrived, Beau was already waiting outside with a single bill of sale in his hand.

He approached the car and motioned for Denney to lower the window, which she did. He handed her the bill of sale from the auction. "Rev. Richard Roundstable bought it. He asked me to call him Vicar Dick, as I recall. I ran the auction about this desk—well, he was the high bidder at $350.00."

Before Denney could say a word, Beau turned on his heel, went back inside his store, and slammed the door. A sign on the front door warned, "Closed for the Day."

"Well, I never," said Denney.

Kat backed up the Mark V and pulled away. "Let's go

pack and shut up the house. We got what we needed. We now know where that desk is. I'm happy to go home to St. James now and see Rusty, and I'm sure you'll be glad to see Gus and Jules too."

The brain fog had cleared, and Kat drove seamlessly through the traffic as Denney sat comfortably in the car.

Denney exclaimed, "We followed some awful lookalike while we were there that awful night in Algiers, and I want to get to the bottom of this... *awfulness*. We *know* it wasn't Ashleigh. I now think it is the twin that Merriweather spoke about."

"Yikes, you could be right. At least we know Ashleigh isn't leading a double life; that would be creepy!"

Kat arranged to have the Mark V sent back to St. James on a flatbed carrier. They paid a lot of cash to AAA for this service, but Kat knew Denney would be a handful driving around in anything else, and that was worth avoiding. She closed the house, and the sisters took a cab to the airport. As usual, she was nearly sprinting to TSA security. She hated being late for boarding.

"Kat, slow down, the gate is just ahead, and we have to make our comfort stop now," reminded Denney.

The departing gate announced boarding, and they were relieved, figuratively and literally, to hop on the plane and head for their favorite home.

Chapter 16

The Dogs Could Smell the Pepperoni

After arriving late on Saturday, Kat slept later than Denney, which was unusual on Sunday, leaving no time for a casual breakfast. She hurried downstairs and spoke quickly to Denney. "I need to leave now so I can catch Ashleigh before the first service starts. He'll still be with the kids until they're released to their parents. So, no hanging around this morning. I need my coffee to go."

"Well, why?" asked Denney.

"Because Ashleigh volunteered to chaperone the youth group for their annual overnight lockdown, and I'm afraid he'll be eager to leave."

"That's fine, Kat," responded Denney. "Take the dogs with you, please; they need to get out some." As she turned to Kat, she added, "Here is your insulated coffee mug. I will go to the second service and perhaps meet up with you there."

Kat clasped the coffee mug, grabbed the leashes for the dogs, and whistled for them to jump into the Vespa. This was a tight squeeze. Rusty sat in her lap, and Gus and Jules were on the passenger seat. The manila envelope was now crushed and jammed under the passenger seat. The car windows were down, and the dogs craned their necks to look and have a smell.

She pulled around the back of the church where the auditorium was and where the kids would be with Ashleigh. Eager to get out of the car, and unleashed, the dogs were all too happy to follow her to the double doors. As she reached the auditorium doors, she checked the dogs, making them sit and be patient before she knocked on the door. A young man came down the hallway, shielding his eyes from the sunny glare through the windows. As he approached, the dogs started barking. They recognized him before she did.

"Hush," she softly commanded.

Rusty stopped barking and sat with his bottom planted firmly on the concrete portico. He waited quietly for a treat. The young man opened the door and was immediately greeted by the dogs.

"Hey, fellas, how are my favorite canines today? Hello to you too, Kat; what brings you here today?" he said jovially.

"Hi, Jeremy, I'm looking for Ashleigh. Has he left yet?"

The Assistant Youth Director at St. Kitt's, Jeremy, pulled out three little milk biscuits from his pocket. One for each dog. He worked at the post office and knew the benefit of always carrying a treat around with him. "Oh, yes, he's still here. He may be back by the dumpsters as we are cleaning up. Lots of empty pizza boxes to get rid of and other such stuff. I would check there first as I think he was headed in that direction."

"Thanks, Jeremy. You're a peach." Kat leashed the dogs while they licked Jeremy's hand. Then they responded to Kat's command to get moving.

As they rounded the corner of the building heading toward the dumpsters, the dogs pulled their leashes, and she forcefully reined them in. "Easy," she commanded.

She was looking down at the dogs and the dogs were looking ahead at Ashleigh, who was leaning against the dumpster with an open pizza box on his lap and a big slice in his hand. The dogs could smell the pepperoni and hamburger, and she knew they could snatch it from Ashleigh without much trouble.

Ashleigh spied the dogs about the same time they saw him. He quickly stood up and threw the empty pizza box over the top of the dumpster. He kept the slice and took off at a dead run. She'd been watching the dogs and was trying to figure out what was going on when the dogs broke away and took up the chase.

Loose leashes whipped after the dogs as they bounded with glee after Ashleigh and his slice. Rusty and Gus being smaller dogs and closer to the ground, poured on the speed. With their bellies almost touching the ground, they started gaining on Ashleigh. Jules was older but had longer legs and was able to stay close to the smaller dogs.

She saw Ashleigh and knew exactly where he was headed, so she didn't worry about losing the dogs. Ashleigh was a big man but could run pretty fast when pressed. But, unless he made it to his destination quickly, the dogs would catch him for sure.

She watched as Ashleigh ran around to the front of the church, where he bounded up the steps and charged through the front doors.

Vicar Dick was looking over his sermon notes when he heard the front doors open and shut. Mildred wasn't there yet, so he decided he ought to check it out. The dogs skidded to a stop at the church doors as he met them.

"Hold it right there, boys. You too, Jules," he said sternly. All three dogs whined with their tongues hanging out as he stood on the front steps looking around. Kat rounded the corner and looked at the dogs, then the vicar.

"You three are mighty lucky you met the vicar and not Mrs. Purvis," said Kat.

"What brings you and the dogs out this early to church?" asked Vicar Dick.

Seeing the vicar was preoccupied as he stood there with his hands on his hips, Kat stated, "If I'm not mistaken, Ashleigh just scooted through these doors. I think he is claiming sanctuary again because of the dogs, and I wanted to talk with him about something."

"For Pete's sake, here we go again. I've talked to Ashleigh about using the church as his hideout, and I bet he's outside in the garden. He knows he cannot use my office as he's often coming from somewhere on a dead run and sweating like crazy."

Vicar Dick went on with some frustration in his voice.

"Then he wants to sit on the furniture, with fans on full tilt blowing my paperwork everywhere and Mrs. Purvis complaining about having to redo the furniture cushions yet again."

He looked at Kat resignedly and offered, "He'll probably be in the garden for at least a couple of hours. That is if he doesn't decide to nap."

"I think I'll just leave him back there and check on him after the second service. I have a feeling he won't be coming out anytime soon. Thanks, Vicar." Kat gathered up the leashes and whistled once again for the dogs to hop into the Vespa.

Once home, she gave the dogs water and let them out to nap in the backyard shade.

Denney looked at the dogs and their beaming faces and said, "I just knew getting out in the fresh air would be good for them. They are so relaxed now. What good dogs they are!"

Kat sighed as she hung up the leashes. Then she told Denney that Ashleigh would be at the church after the second service, and they could catch up with him then to find out more about his twin.

"I was interrupted by Vicar Dick, and I felt I couldn't talk with Ashleigh then because he was already worked up after the dog chase."

"Dog chase? How interesting! But that sounds perfect," Denney said cheerily. "I'm so glad Ashleigh is taking part in church activities and is willing to spend so much time there. It can only do him good, I think."

Kat agreed and went upstairs to get ready for church.

After changing her clothes, she returned to the kitchen where Denney was waiting, finishing her coffee. Kat was dressed in casual but expensive black slacks with a loose-fitting tailored creamy white blouse. She was wearing red flats for a pop of color.

"You look very nice," said Denney as she inspected Kat before they left. "I couldn't have dressed you better myself."

As they walked to church, Kat filled Denney in on the chase at church earlier that morning.

"No wonder the fur-babies were pooped," allowed Denney.

As they neared the front of St. Kitts, Kat remembered the manila envelope that should have been on the passenger floor of the Vespa. She and Denney would have to have a conversation about the contents of that envelope as it remained a mystery. They also had to catch Ashleigh after the service to see if he knew the whereabouts of his brother.

They also needed to have a conversation with Vicar Dick about the desk purchased from Beau Buford's auction and where it was stored. They could not corner the Vicar on Sunday morning as he was busily looking over his sermon notes and did not wish to be disturbed. So many unanswered questions. She decided not to have too much pre-communion wine this morning to stay sharp.

She had volunteered at the church to retrieve the wine

from the cupboard and usually had a couple of hardy sips before it was blessed and used for the congregation. She figured she might only be able to have one this time as she needed to focus.

The sisters entered the church and sat in their customary pew.

During the sermon, Kat thought she saw some movement through the stained-glass window overlooking the garden. She started to cough as an excuse to leave the service. As others around her began to look annoyed, she stood up and made her way down the pew, toward the aisle, and then to the narthex.

She hurried out the front doors and around the building, turning left where the garden wall began. She had at one time, in her long career of professions, studied to become a master gardener. She loved the old brick wall covered by an old, rambling forsythia, which had largely overtaken the area. She thought that perhaps she could come and do a little pruning in the future. But for now, it provided good cover to peer over the top. She stretched her five-foot-three-inch frame until she could just see over and through the hedge.

Ashleigh paced around the garden. He seemed to be anxious, which for him signaled an imminent departure.

Kat quietly went to the front of the church and sent a text to Denney. "He's going to run—come on."

Denney's phone was on vibrate and had fallen deep into her purse. Desperate to silence the purring phone and not being able to lay her hands on it, she hurriedly left the church, rummaging through her purse all the way. She barreled out the front doors, and saw Kat waiting for her. "What is it?" she asked?

"Didn't you read my text?"

"I couldn't find my cell in my purse, so I left before the vibrating gave folks the wrong idea," said Denney sarcastically.

"You think those guys would make the connection? For years, most of those women have had an 'out of business' sign attached to their clothes. I even think they have a women's group named in that same way, and I think I saw it in the church bulletin."

Denney looked at her skeptically.

"What?!" Kat responded.

Denney asked, "Is there really such a group?"

Kat replied over her shoulder as she walked toward the garden, "Anyway, Ashleigh is pacing, and I'm sure he is going to take it on the arches. Do you want to talk with him now?"

Denney squinted at Kat and asked, "What does 'taking it on the arches' mean?"

Kat looked at Denney incredulously and replied, "Beat feet, of course!"

"Okay then," replied Denney, "I'm beatin' feet'."

Kat shook her head and said, "My God, Denney, don't you even read?"

They moved quickly to the outside garden gate. Surely, they agreed, he wouldn't go back into the church now. They were right. Ashleigh quietly closed the garden's wrought iron gates behind him as he turned to see Kat and Denney standing squarely in front of him.

"Oh, dear me," squeaked Ashleigh. "I didn't expect to see you. What a *surprise!*"

"Relax!" said Denney. "You're as skittery as a cat on a hot tin roof." Denney smiled at her response, knowing that it was not original but fitting at the same time.

Kat took in Ashleigh's appearance and felt sorry for him. Pizza sauce had splattered on the front of his shirt. "We were informed that you had a brother—a twin. But we thought we saw *you* in Algiers and that you might be leading a double life." Straightening herself to her full height, she continued. "Could we be wrong? Can you shed any light on this?"

Ashleigh looked at Denney, then quickly looked at Kat. He was uncomfortable and began to sweat more heavily. His stiff shirt became limp, and the odor of Jade East was overpowering. On Jeremy's advice, Ashleigh had taken to wearing copious amounts of both Jade East cologne and deodorant. It was finally apparent that Ashleigh had no sense of smell.

He appeared afraid and didn't seem to want to talk to them about anything.

Turning to Denney, he said, "Miss Lindene, I would rather not burden you with the tawdry history of my twin brother. I would rather you think well of me, and I am quite sure telling you anything about Winfield would tarnish your opinion of me by association. Please don't make me recall any childhood history with my brother."

Denney eyed Ashleigh and said, "Look, in ten words or less, what kind of person is Winfield?"

Kat smiled at Ashleigh and motioned him to continue.

Ashleigh squared his shoulders, took a deep breath, cleared his throat, and began, "He was at Strangeways, a prison in Manchester for the most dangerous. He escaped but left behind a cellmate named Asmond. From Winfield's letters, he led me to believe that Asmond was a bad, bad man. Winfield had last written to me he needed some money as he could not take the chance of securing it himself. You know, I am on a stipend—a spendthrift trust—as it were. He said he had some plans for his friend, Asmond, and while Asmond was much feared in the prison community, he certainly could not hold a candle to my brother's intellect and that my brother planned to use Asmond in some sort of way. I wrote Winfield and told him that I couldn't send him anything. I felt bad."

Kat looked intently at Ashleigh, "Do you know if Winfield has been in Louisville lately?

"I don't know," Ashleigh said apologetically.

Ashleigh looked at both sisters. There was a pleading in his eyes. Denney saw this and said, "Do you know why he was in prison?

"Not really. No one ever spoke of it."

"Ashleigh, you have been most helpful," said Kat.

"It's much appreciated. We'll see you soon."

Kat could tell Ashleigh was ready to ask when that might happen. She cut him off. "Ashleigh, you look exhausted and in need of a good bath. Why don't you run along? I assure you we will be contacting you soon."

Kat paused with her hand still resting on the garden gate. She said to Denney, "Well, we didn't know that Winfield existed. Except for Ashleigh, the Daggits were not on our radar. If it hadn't been for St. Kitts, Ashleigh would have been unknown to us as well." she said thoughtfully.

"What an interesting turn of events," replied Denney.

"Isn't it really! This concerns me for Ashleigh's safety, especially since his brother has been in prison, for Pete's sake!" Kat said with alarm.

"We need to keep this in mind," agreed Denney.

Ashleigh looked a little disappointed yet hopeful. He started to make his way home while the sisters walked, arm in arm, back to St. James to let the dogs out and relax until evening cocktails.

***

As Ashleigh left the garden, the conversation left him feeling vulnerable and confused. He wondered if his brother could be nearby. Instead of walking home, he once again strolled up the front stairs of St. Kitts and headed to Vicar Dick's office. The vicar, who had just finished the last morning service, was hanging up his vestments. Ashleigh walked in unannounced, startling the vicar.

"Oh, darn it, Ashleigh, you need to knock or something."

"Vicar, I need to talk with you. I mean, I need to talk with you." Ashleigh was so red-faced that Vicar Dick was alarmed.

"Sit down, Ashleigh. Pour yourself some water from the carafe there on the side table."

The vicar looked at him sternly but with a little more concern than usual. "Ashleigh, I'm here for you. Just take a breath. I'm not going anywhere."

As he waited for Ashleigh to begin, he turned on the small fan directly behind him to deflect the overpowering Jade East.

Ashleigh whispered, looking furtively at the vicar, said in a breathy voice, "Help me."

Vicar Dick was concerned and nodded affirmatively.

Ashleigh explained to the vicar that he felt his brother was near, may be back in town. He didn't know how, but Kat and Denney saw him in Algiers just a few days ago. He explained how the sisters thought Winfield was him and questioned him about it. "That scares me—that they would think I was bad. I told the sisters Winfield had written to me that he needed some money and had asked to stay with me—just last week."

Vicar Dick realized he had in his possession documents that would prove that Winfield, Ashleigh's twin brother, was also related to Kat and Denney.

Vicar Dick sat back in his desk chair and addressed

Ashleigh softly. "Ashleigh, what do you know about your brother?"

"What do you mean… I mean… he's my brother, but he went to boarding school and stayed there from fifth grade on. I guess we aren't much like brothers, and I don't recall seeing much of him after that."

"What did your parents tell you about this boarding school?" quizzed the vicar.

"Well, they said Winfield was very, very smart and that the schools here couldn't help him develop his mind like the boarding school could. We were proud of him. I missed him at first, but then he was away so long…" Ashleigh trailed off and looked over the vicar and through the window behind him.

"What are you thinking about, now?"

"I sort of remember playing with Winfield. He was a good runner, and we played catch in the school yard. When he would throw the ball to me, I couldn't catch it. It hit me all the time. One day the ball hit me on the side of my head." Ashleigh motioned to his right temple. "Mother was angry. I tried to tell her I tried to catch the ball, but I wasn't fast enough. I remember Mother saying, 'I've had enough.' I didn't mean to get him into trouble."

The vicar took off his glasses, rubbed his eyes, and sighed. Looking up at Ashleigh, he said, "Ashleigh, you are a grown man, but you're too kind, and you live a simple life. You've been sheltered all these years from the truth about your brother, and now I want to help you understand something for your own good."

"Do you mean that Winfield has been in prison? I know that."

"Not exactly. Winfield was and perhaps still should be in prison. The truth is that Winfield has significant mental and emotional problems. He's barely stable with his medication. Without it, *he is* paranoid and dangerous. He did go to boarding school for a couple of years. In fact, he's brilliant. But, by the time he was in his early teens, it was apparent that he was psychopathic. He was in and out of institutions and boarding schools until he turned eighteen.

I'm afraid that psychiatric care for those with these problems is sorely lacking, and Winfield was on his own. Your parents tried to help by giving him a living allowance and paying for his medical care.

Predictably, Winfield wound up with the wrong crowd and ended up in prison. Your parents loved him until the day they passed. But finally, when he went to prison, they gave up trying to help him."

Ashleigh had a faraway look in his eyes. "I suppose I knew things weren't exactly like Mother told me, but I never believed Winfield would hurt anyone. I want to help him."

"NO," exclaimed the vicar. "I mean, please... stay away from him and stay out of his life. I've told you this before. Now I've shared why. Winfield doesn't feel the same emotions that you and I feel. You can't reason with him or appeal to a sense of caring. He feels no remorse. Do you understand?"

Ashleigh sat silently.

"Do you understand? Look at me. Do you understand what I'm saying?"

Ashleigh looked up. His big blue eyes were clouded over, but he wiped away any tears before they could fall. "Yes," he replied softly.

As Ashleigh left the office, the vicar's mind was racing with all the stories and confessions that he had been privy to over the years. He was the repository of many private confidences. How could he let people know only as much as they needed to be safe and secure without betraying those who trusted him to safeguard their secrets? He was disturbed that Winfield was free and out and about. He felt a great deal of concern for Ashleigh's welfare and wondered what Winfield might be plotting.

That was the one part of being a priest that he thoroughly disliked. He knew too much and could often do too little. He thought about all the times he saw the Daggit family at church. They appeared to be an all-American family. But Mr. Daggit was busy building his own empire. Daggit confided to him that he loved his boys and would do anything for them, but it just seemed easier if it involved money. He was just so often preoccupied. It was clear that the boys longed for more attention as they idolized their father. But Winfield resented his father and seemed to learn early that money was the overriding expression of love and his measure as a man.

Chapter 17

Should I be a Pre-School Teacher?

Kat shouted from the kitchen, "Great, you're up! I've had coffee, but I'm making our lattes."

"Awesome." Denney knew Kat was making herself a latte, and since she heard her coming downstairs, she made the offer plural.

In a pair of jeans, a t-shirt, and her new gray Vans, Kat was ready to go. Her hair was tucked under her NASA ball cap.

"Okay, what's up?" questioned Denney.

Denney noticed Kat was a touch on the nervy side after so much coffee, and Kat used the word "actually" a lot when she was overstimulated. Denney suggested she walk to the church as it might be safer for her and those on the road with her.

"Absolutely," Kat replied as she jumped up from the chair and headed for the door with Rusty following and dragging his leash. She made her way down the front porch steps and quickly turned in the direction of the church. Rusty followed with the handhold of the leash in his mouth to decrease the drag until Kat noticed him.

Denney yawned, shook her head in amazement and headed back in the house to dress for the day.

As Kat reached the church, she realized she had forgotten Rusty. As she turned around to go back and get him, she almost stumbled over him while he patiently waited behind her. He dropped the leash handle and sat down.

"Well, would you look at you!" cooed Kat.

Rusty's little butt and stub tail wiggled in response. Kat picked up the leash, and they both made their way inside the church back towards the church office.

Vicar Dick heard them coming as he could recognize Kat's voice from her conversation with Rusty. "Hello, Kat, and good morning to you. I see you have Rusty with you. Would you like a little water, fella?" As he secured a bowl of water for Rusty, he asked Kat if she had driven today.

"Actually, no. Too much coffee this morning, so I thought I would walk, actually."

"Great, that allows us to put Denney's recent contribution to work on something other than buying more sod," said Vicar Dick. "I have some paperwork I want to share with you if you have time?"

"I do!" Kat responded cheerily. She instructed Rusty to sit, making herself comfortable in the office chair across from the vicar's desk. As Kat waited for Vicar Dick to seat himself, she noted how precisely his desk was laid out with stacks of papers.

"My goodness, you sure look busy this morning. Your desk is just full of work. All those congregants needing attention, I guess. You know, actually, I was thinking of doing some work with a group of youngsters, and I was wondering if you thought my future desk might be as laden with paperwork as yours?" Kat inquired a little too loudly.

Vicar Dick leaned back in his desk chair and studied her. "I don't think I can answer that. I do, however, want to bring to your attention some rather astounding paperwork I found that reveals some information about Ashleigh and Winfield Daggit that will certainly be of interest to you and Denney." He moved his hand over the stacks until it rested on the one he searched for. He pulled out a manila envelope that had a striking resemblance to the one she had misplaced.

"Ahh, I have it here," he proclaimed as he carefully laid it before Kat. "The Colonel asked me to look into some old Baptismal records and make a copy of some family information and send it to him. I did. Then I received this in the mail. It was the same baptismal record I sent him but with some handwritten notes in the margin. Amazing, isn't it? I can tell Ashleigh if you wish," offered Vicar Dick.

He noticed some alarm on Kat's face. "You didn't get the copy the Colonel sent you, did you? Judging from your behavior, I would venture to guess you have not."

Puzzled, she took up the manila envelope, noticing that it was identical to the one they received and misplaced. She pulled out the stapled sheets of paper to read them. "Denney is gonna' freak," she gasped.

"Yes, I thought so too," Vicar Dick said merrily as he enjoyed sparring with Denney.

"Does Ashleigh know about this, that we're related?" asked Kat.

The vicar deflected her question about Ashleigh and replied, "The Colonel knew of the family ties and called me sometime before his death to ask me to confirm some information he had come across. Now you know it as well."

As Kat studied the papers, Vicar Dick thought about his days in the seminary and his first assignment to St. Kitts when he met the Colonel. The Colonel, who was only a few years older, was drawn to Dick's good-natured sense of humor and wry wit.

The Colonel, a spiritual man but without any trappings of religiosity, found Dick easy to talk with. He often invited Dick to the Jeffersonian for a few drinks and lively, wide-ranging conversation. After seminary and being a newly minted reverend, Dick accepted a position as associate rector at a church in Houston. When Vicar Jim retired, and the diocese posted an opening at St. Kitt's, Dick submitted his name for consideration.

The Colonel, who attended Sunday services and nothing more, told Dick he had approached Ed Conklin, the senior warden of the vestry, and had asked to be appointed to the search committee. The colonel enjoyed telling how he laughed when he saw how shocked and mystified Ed was. The Colonel also bragged that he used his family, stalwarts of the church reaching back generations, to seal the deal. Ed had replied to the Colonel that he would submit his name to the vestry.

As the Colonel expected, the vestry agreed that he would add a fresh voice to the search committee and wanted to encourage him to take a more significant role in the church's life. The Colonel was well-respected, primarily due to his family ties, but he was not well-known as an individual.

Having made the short list, with the Colonel's support, Dick sailed through the interview with the committee, and Ed called him and asked him to serve the church.

Vicar Dick paused his memories, shifted in his chair, leaned forward, placed his folded hands-on top of his desk, and cleared his throat.

Kat shuffled her papers into a neat stack and looked at Vicar Dick. "Is there anything else I need to know?"

He took the papers, squared the edges neatly, and continued, "No, nothing I can think of."

"Actually, I think I need to talk with Denney about this before we move on that," Kat replied.

Vicar Dick eyed her with a certain amount of glee and stated, "That would probably be wise. Is there anything else I can do for you today?"

"Well, yes," she said, "actually, I'm here because Denney wanted me to ask you about a piece of furniture that you bought from an auction at Beau Buford's Bypass Furniture and Auction in New Orleans."

The vicar looked surprised. "I had completely forgotten about that. I can do that easily. As I recall, I received a telephone call from the Colonel. He was arguing with his landlady in New Orleans about a rent payment for a lady friend of his. He said he could prove he had paid it, although the Landlady was alleging that he had not, so she was auctioning the flat's contents for back rent.

He asked me, fervently, to purchase his desk, part of the contents—for any amount—and said that he would pay me back—which he did, I might add. It was the only thing he wanted, and he asked me to hold on to it. He was no longer in a relationship with the woman in the apartment, and she just dropped off the map. So, I flew to New Orleans, bought the desk at auction, and brought it here. It's been in the attic since just before the Colonel's untimely death. Certainly, if it is something you want, it's yours. If you're not interested, I can find a home for it somewhere."

Kat was half-listening as she continued to mull over how to tell Denney about the Daggits and the desk. She looked at Vicar Dick. "Of course, we want it. I'll talk with Denney and make arrangements for it to be sent to the house." Her coffee was wearing off, and she was eager to get back home and share the news.

"I assume I can take this paperwork with me?" asked Kat. She grabbed the manila envelope and stuffed the paperwork back inside.

"Of course," said Vicar Dick. "Have a great rest of the day, Kat, and knowing Denney, she'll find this news shocking. It will allow me to tease her a bit, and that is a great gift today. You know what they say about paying it forward," he chuckled. I will look forward to chatting with you and Denney should you feel the need to unburden yourselves."

Rusty slurped up the rest of the water from his bowl and followed her out of the office, dragging his leash again as she studied the paperwork again on the way home. She just couldn't believe it.

Kat arrived quickly. As she purposefully made her way up the front steps, she called for Denney, who was on the back porch reading the newspaper. Rusty ran to the back door to greet her. Denney, hearing him, entered the kitchen to unleash him and let him out as he was eager to rid himself of all the water he had drunk at Vicar Dick's.

"DENNEY!" Kat called loudly, "Come here quickly!"

Denney hated to be startled like that. "You better be dying," she shouted back.

Kat said, "I think you'd better sit down for this one."

"Shall I make Manhattans first?" she quipped.

"Yeah, but this is serious." Kat sat at the kitchen island with the manila envelope in front of her.

As Denney mixed the Manhattans, she saw the envelope and asked her, "Is that the envelope from your car?"

Kat responded, "Oh shit!" slid off her stool and dashed off to her car. When she opened the car door, she frantically searched the passenger side floorboard. She reached under the passenger seat and found a crumpled envelope wedged under the seat. It was covered with dog hair and half-eaten

Bourbon & Benjamins

dog biscuits but was otherwise intact.

Denney had already started sipping her Manhattan and eyeing the envelope Kat had just picked up from Vicar Dick. She muttered, "Oh, the hell with it!" and opened it. She pulled out two Xeroxed pages of old-fashioned color print. At the top, it read "Baptismal Records of St. Kitts Episcopal Parish." Reading on, she saw "Daggit" in the first column to the left, then the date February 28, 1905, in the next column, and then "Parents" in the third column: Wilson and Madeline Daggit and finally the Baptized infant's name: Charles Emmitt Daggit. Denney looked at the handwritten notes "second wife, Vivian Whaley, daughter Catherine Daggit. Marriage of Catherine to Marvin Kincaid" Denney was shocked.

As Denney wondered what the relevance of this was, Kat barged through the door, waving a wrinkled manila envelope in her hand. She looked at Denney and girded herself for an explosion. "Denney, have you read any of that yet?" Denney did not respond, and Kat hurriedly went on. "I have here the envelope you asked about and because I know what the first envelope contains, this second envelope has originals in it! The very same information. Denney?"

Denney looked up and said, "I need to check some old papers." Denney ran upstairs and retrieved a small wooden box. Inside was an old family Bible. She grabbed it and went downstairs. "Kat, something triggered this in my mind."

She flipped pages to the center of the Bible, where

births and other events were written in longhand. There was a notation showing the marriage of Vivian Josephine Whaley to Charles Emmet Daggit. As she ran her finger down the page, she discovered the birth of a daughter to Vivian and Wilson. The daughter was Catherine. Both Kat and Denney gasped. Catherine Daggit was their great-grandmother!

Kat downed her Manhattan without coming up for air. They never knew their great-grandmother's maiden name was Daggit. "Well, that settles it. It's true. Just as Vicar Dick said, we are related to Ashleigh Daggit. Do you think we can get a loan somehow?" she said with some light sarcasm.

Kat asked Denney, "Do you think Ashleigh knows this? We need to do some investigating,"

At that, Denney choked on her Manhattan.

"I don't know if he does or not. He never answered that question. So far, you, me, and Vicar Dick are the only ones aware of this at the moment," said Kat as she poured herself another drink. "Anyway, let's sit on it for now. We need to continue to look for our inheritance."

Denney agreed to sit on the information for now and the sisters made their way upstairs to bed with much on their minds.

Chapter 18

I Truly Love It

That morning, Denney opened the garage door with her clicker and found she couldn't open the driver's side of the Mark V. She walked around to the passenger side, grumbling about Kat's collection of gardening tools she recently purchased and not stored away. Kat's mess caused her to crawl over her own stack of interior decorator magazines and press the button that would send the driver's seat back.

Once she had a little more clearance, she could kneel in the seat and then twist around, facing front behind the steering wheel, sliding across the chamois leather seats pulled at her slacks, causing her to have to arch her back to pull them back around. She had started to perspire in the hot car in the hot garage, and her travel mug of coffee no longer looked good.

She wedged her travel mug between a couple of stacks of home and decor magazines for safekeeping. She placed her phone in the glove box. She loved her old Mark V and was willing to adjust for its lack of more modern accessories like a cup holder in the console. Finally settled, she started the car and turned the air conditioning to the *max.* As she pulled out of the garage, her anxiety about the information discussed with Kat the night before took over.

Denney remembered Kat's remark about the Junk Bully and decided to see if he would be available to move the desk from Vicar Dick's attic to their house. She headed that way. Soon Denney pulled onto the disintegrating concrete parking lot adjoining the store. She checked her hair, blotted her face, and slid reluctantly out of the car.

The Junk Bully was open. A rusty bell dinged as she opened the door. A teenage girl approached her, wearing jeans with cut-out knees and a gray tee stretched across her ample mid-section. She had a sleeve of tattoos on her left arm. Her chin-length raven-black hair kept falling in front of her eyes. "Yeah?" she said.

Denney was taken aback. What? No, *"May I help you?"* or even *"We're not open yet"* as a greeting, she thought, but she managed a smile and said she wanted to see the proprietor.

The girl responded, "B.W.F. don't want to see you."

Denney bristled at the impertinence of this unknown girl. "Okay, I haven't met you. You seem lovely, but I need to see… B.W.F.? Do you pronounce that Bwiff?"

The girl glanced over her shoulder and saw B.W.F. looking at them. Denney followed her glance and saw him too. Not interested in more exchanges with the girl, she brushed past her and walked to the store's back.

B.W.F. looked Denney up and down, "Just what may I do for you, madam?"

"Well, good morning to you, Mr. Bwiff. My sister mentioned that you know Vicar Dick. We have a piece of furniture that he is holding for us, but he can't move it as it is rather large and heavy. Moving companies don't take these small jobs except for an exorbitant price. Since Vicar Dick recommended you, how much would it cost to move it four blocks for me? Plus, I will call him so he will be ready to assist you."

B.W.F. thoughtfully considered the proposal as he needed some ready cash, and even though he heard the sisters were a crazy-ass pair of women, he decided to run the risk. "I could move it for you for the right price," he said.

Denney didn't want to let social niceties get in the way of a simple deal, so she said, "How about gas and $300? That would cover an hour's work."

"Three seventy-five, cash," he countered.

"Agreed," Denney said testily. Be at the church at ten a.m. tomorrow. The vicar will be there. If you need extra help, someone will be around to assist. I assume you will be the one to help move it and not your girl assistant?"

B.W.F. responded, "Doing a man's work, though a child at heart... we wouldn't want *that* now would we?"

Denney considered him carefully, "Mr. Bwiff, there may be more to you than meets the eye."

Denney left the Junk Bully and motored home to find Kat putting away her new gardening equipment in the garage. She exited the car from the driver's side and said,

"I have arranged for Mr. Bwiff at the Junk Bully to deliver our desk after pick-up at the church tomorrow." She also filled her in on the exceptional deal made on their behalf to save money.

"His name is Bwiff?" asked Kat.

"I believe so. Anyway, he quoted Robert Frost, which I find to be interesting. I am going to try and find out a little more about him later. Maybe he would be a possible addition to my poet's group. Of course, he would have to clean himself up and do something with that hair. You were right about that hair of his."

Kat lifted her glass of iced tea from the work bench and peered over the top. "Is that what you got out of my question about his name?"

Denney looked at her blankly.

Kat shrugged and picked up more tools to take to the potting shed. "You actually drove the Mark V by yourself?" Kat asked in amazement.

***

Back at the Junk Bully, Byron Whitman Frost sent his niece home and enjoyed an ice-cold glass of water while reading "The First Kiss of Love" by Lord Byron and thinking of Denney.

Bwiff arrived the next day, on time at St. Kitt's. The vicar and Ashleigh located the desk in the attic, covered in dust. The vicar asked Ashleigh to find some cleaning rags. Ashleigh hurried to the front of the church to ask Mildred for them.

He interrupted Mildred's phone conversation to ask for supplies, and she shushed him and pointed to a closet in her office where he found them.

Bwiff pulled up in the moving van. He casually walked into the church office where Ashleigh was now juggling an armful of paper towels and spray bottles.

"Where are we headed?" Bwiff asked Ashleigh good-naturedly. "Do you need some help there?" As he watched Ashleigh barely keep hold of his supplies.

"No, that's okay, I've got it," Ashleigh assured him. In the next moment, all the supplies tumbled to the floor. In his anxiety, he started to sweat.

Mildred watched as the bottle of cleaner split open and sprayed her cherished rubber tree plant... a present from Vicar Dick two Christmases ago.

Ashleigh turned pale, and Bwiff gasped at the expression on Mildred's face.

Mildred's only shocked response was, "DAMN IT!"

Bwiff and Ashleigh quickly picked up the damaged cleaning supplies as Mildred screamed, "OUT, OUT, OUT!"

Bwiff was getting frustrated. "Let's get started moving that desk. I need to get back to the store."

***

The doorbell rang just before lunch. Kat was in the kitchen loading the dishwasher, and Denney was out back with the dogs, watching them run and enjoying the afternoon. Kat's hands were wet, so she yelled out to her through the open French door. "Denney, it seems that someone is ringing the doorbell. Can you get it? I'm loading the dishwasher."

"Be right there," answered Denney as she whistled to the dogs to come in. As she made her way to the front door, the bell chimed again. It was Vicar Dick with his finger poised over the bell. She stood aside as he made his way into the foyer. He gazed around and directed Ashleigh and B.W.F. to bring the desk in and leave it there. B.W.F. glanced at her and gave a nod and a smile.

Ashleigh noticed the attention of B.W.F. toward her and announced, "Oh, have you met my dear friend, Lindene? We are so close. Have been for years."

Vicar Dick looked curiously at Denney and asked, "*My*, I didn't know you and Ashleigh were so close."

Denney studied Ashleigh with immense fascination but decided not to say anything.

Ashleigh's eyes went wide with apprehension at Denney's silence. "We have known each other for some time, I am sure of that," repeated Ashleigh nervously.

Kat strolled out to see how the delivery was going, noticing Ashleigh mopping the sweat from his brow, and offered the men iced tea and scones.

"Thank you, that was very generous—no, I won't stay for tea—I know Mrs. Purvis is waiting on me. "Those look like her scones, are they?" asked the vicar.

Kat smiled. "They sure are. Want to take one with you

for later?"

"Don't mind if I do," said Vicar Dick. He neatly wrapped the scone in a linen napkin, offered him by Denney, and made his way to the door. She caught him on the front porch and handed him a sealed envelope. Vicar Dick slit open the envelope and found several hundred dollars inside.

"Why, thank you, Denney, your support is always appreciated and much needed," he said.

Kat dispatched B.W.F. and Ashleigh back inside the house with a couple of scones, and red plastic go cups of iced tea.

B.W.F. passed Denney on the porch, and as he was leaving, he once again smiled her way and waved goodbye.

Ashleigh, girding himself for her judgment, gave her a wide berth.

Denney reentered the house where Kat had a tall etched-crystal glass of iced tea waiting for her. Denney stood back with her arms crossed and assessed the desk. They both looked at the desk that now sat in the middle of the foyer. Denney stood back and started to evaluate out loud the merits of the desk.

"You know, Kat, it's made of pecan wood, such a rich color. The legs are a little wobbly and will have to be tightened. But, oh look at them, they are carved like cobra heads." She ran her hands over the top of the desk and exclaimed, "Inlaid pieces of exotic wood, how lovely. It just keeps getting better. The drawer pulls appear to be carved from bone, perhaps ivory, each with two elephant heads. Their trunks meet in the middle. I think I could swoon. *I truly love it!*" said Denney in a hushed tone.

Kat studied the desk as well. "I agree. It's a simply delicious and gorgeous piece of furniture."

"I feel a connection to it already. Don't you, Kat?"

"Yeah, I really do."

The desk sat there for the rest of the afternoon while they discussed how best to refurbish it and where they would put it before retiring to the porch for their private happy hour.

"I'm worried," said Kat. "Our inheritance is just something we have to restore. Maybe we should just start looking for jobs."

"Perhaps it's a pipe dream. Maybe there isn't anything else. I just don't think I'm cut out to look for a job. I'm not sure what that even really means," Denney said tiredly.

The sun began to set and throw patterned shadows on Denney's tasteful seating arrangement.

They both sighed just a little.

Now in their pajamas, housecoats, and slippers, they ceremoniously carried a dog each upstairs to bed. Jules followed, and it was time to catch up on their reading and, if their blood pressure allowed, the news.

Chapter 19

Writers, Poets, and Artists

Thursday morning was cloudy, with a smell of rain in the air. Kat was making her latte and having no end of trouble with her frothier. While flipping its switch and occasionally banging it on the countertop, she casually said she thought the Junk Bully might have a crush on her.

Denney huffed, "Why would you conjure up such a thing this early in the morning? That's just nonsense. He and I have absolutely nothing in common except for the fact that he reads. WHOOPEE!"

Kat stuck her frothier under the faucet, trying to get it to work. "Now, why would you think I would make that up?"

"To annoy me—why else?"

"Why would that annoy you?"

"Because people like him live in another world. Writers, poets, artists, psychologists—they all have one foot on the ground and the other in a pool of tears."

Kat stared at Denney for a second and replied, "That's sort of cynical, don't you think?" Fully annoyed and exasperated, she tossed the frothier in the trash.

"Ahhh, my dear sister, it's just one of life's lessons that one learns the hard way."

Thinking that the "hard way" probably could relate to this situation, Kat changed the direction of the conversation. "A*nyhoo*, I thought maybe it's time to scale down. I can't imagine trying to keep up with this old house and the one in New Orleans at our age," she responded.

Denney immediately looked shocked. "What, how could we ever replace this house in our lives, in our souls?"

"Not so fast there, maybe we could rent it or somehow keep it—I don't know. All I know is that it is beginning to be too much, mostly because we have a money problem. We've been frugal in some matters, never had a gardener or a housekeeper. I never thought that anyone could do as good a job," Kat added. Yet, she knew their extravagances were widely known.

"Wait!" said Denney, "Are we missing the point or what? I don't believe the desk is all there is. That's not the Colonel's style. When we find this inheritance, we can hire help until the day we pass on to our reward, whatever that might be. Until this discovery of an inheritance, we just never had the means to consider hiring help; now we can!"

Kat thought and finally answered, "As sole survivors, we really don't know how much our inheritance might be. What if we end up needing to be in a retirement home or worse?"

"There may be complications with the Daggits. I have

to see how far removed they might be from the Colonel. I am going to the library to research our genealogy. I would hate to deal with complications in court." Denney said decidedly, "I don't know what I may find, but what will be, will be. All we can do now is get on with our day."

Kat got up from her chair, stretched, and reached down and patted Rusty on his head. She stood up straight with her hands on her hips and said, "Rusty and I are going to see Mrs. Merriweather, and I think you said you were going to the library. Do you need a ride?"

Denney thought that researching Wilson Daggit wouldn't be easy online and decided to visit the main public library. Since parking would be difficult, especially in the Mark V, she humbled herself and asked Kat to drop her off in the Vespa on her way to Merriweather's.

Kat was amused and said she would.

Denney entered the Vespa in the garage out of plain sight and asked Kat to drop her off in the alley, which she did. Then she walked across York Street and through the main entrance.

After a few questions, she found archived newspapers dating to the 1920s.

She was surprised it didn't take exceedingly long to find some information on Wilson Daggit. It was a blessing that while Wilson was heavily invested in the stock market, he was practically clairvoyant, as well. He liquidated almost all his stock, keeping Coca-Cola, U.S. Steel, and American Tobacco just before the crash in 1929. Then he invested in real estate. Optimists on Wall Street thought he was misguided. But Daggit, a purist, felt that overly liberal credit policies couldn't be good. She discovered that Wilson Daggit passed on sizeable real estate holdings and stocks to his heirs and their heirs. Wilson was married twice, not uncommon for the time. His first wife, Madelyn, continued the Daggit line with male heirs. His second wife, Vivian, continued the Daggit line, albeit through female heirs. Wilson treated the female descendants equally with the male descendants.

The Colonel had descended from the female heir, Catherine Daggit. Denney was entranced with her reading. It seemed that she and Kat were third cousins to Ashley and Winfield! She looked up only because her neck was beginning to ache. Standing in the front lobby, she was surprised to see the Ashleigh lookalike, who she now believed had to be Winfield, Ashleigh's twin brother. He was with another man she didn't know. She slumped in her chair so as not to be recognized, with a newspaper shielding her face.

Winfield entered the library with his lackey. Winfield appeared determined and abruptly called to his companion, "Asmond, keep up the pace." They didn't notice Denney or that she was watching them as she peeked around her newspaper.

Winfield asked one of the librarians where the historic deeds were kept. She motioned him to the next counter.

The librarian at the next counter told them in an uncharacteristically loud whisper, "You are not in the right place. These deeds are copies of those original, historic

1700 era land grants but nothing from the 1920s."

Winfield looked angry. "But that woman just told me... oh, never mind. I suppose we need to visit the deed room at the courthouse." Winfield turned to leave, motioning for Asmond to follow. He was ruffled that he was not in the right office to shed some light on family real estate holdings.

Denney waited for the two to exit and then approached the librarian. "Excuse me," she whispered, "what were the two gentlemen looking for?" The librarian paused. Denney didn't know if she was trying to keep the answer a secret or was debating whether they were gentlemen.

"Oh, they were looking for old deeds, just not the really old historic deeds we keep here."

Denney thanked the librarian and made a mental note, and decided she had enough background to share with Kat for the day.

Chapter 20

Purple Velvet Lining

Kat pulled up in front of Mrs. Merriweather's home and noticed a black wreath on the door with a black spray-painted banner announcing the death of Peter the Parrot. She knew the bird was old, but she didn't expect this.

Kat stopped before ringing the bell, patted Rusty on the head, and told him not to gloat. She gave the bell a quick tap and waited patiently on the front stoop for Mrs. Merriweather to open the door. While she waited, she shuffled job opportunities in her head, potentials that she might be interested in pursuing, and none came to mind.

A tearful Mrs. Merriweather opened the door and embraced her. "I'm so glad you have come to see me in my time of grief, and look there, Rusty is with you! Petey's best friend in all the world."

Kat sized up the situation quickly. Mrs. Merriweather was smashed. "I am sooo sorry for your loss, and so is Denney. Is there anything that we can do to help you through this?" she asked.

"Come in, come in, Kat. I am planning an elaborate funeral for Petey. Only the best. I have been looking for a coffin suitable for him. I found an old humidor of the Colonel's, and it's very nice. Real burled wood and a plush purple velvet lining. It fits Petey to a tee. Could you help me with Vicar Dick and the funeral? I so want him to have a graveside service with some of the people he loved. Oh, of course, Rusty too."

Kat was served a coffee with rum as Mrs. Merriweather enlisted her help.

"I'd be glad to help you. What is this about a humidor of the Colonel's?"

"Oh, Kat, I hope you won't be upset! He left it for me to give to you girls, but it's just a cigar holder, and I thought it was perfect for Petey. Are you angry?"

Kat looked at the grief-stricken Mrs. Merriweather and assured her that it would be just fine to bury Petey in such style. Mrs. Merriweather was relieved and fixed her another coffee with rum.

As she and Mrs. Merriweather were on their third rum and coffee, Merriweather asked if Denney might send out the funeral notices to those she wished to have in attendance. Kat assured her that Denney would be honored to do so.

"You and Denney are such good friends, Kat. I don't know what I would do without you," she said, choking up.

"Oh, by the way, what do you think of me becoming a preschool teacher, Merriweather?

Mrs. Merriweather put down her coffee cup and paused for a few moments. "May I suggest that perhaps you reconsider?"

Kat poured more rum into her existing coffee. "How hard can it be?"

She left Merriweather's house with a "to do" list and was escorted home by Rusty. Denney was waiting on the front porch with the usual. Kat slouched into her wicker chair and reached for her drink as Denney looked up from her iPad.

"Hey, I just got back from Mrs. Merriweather's. Petey died! She's going to bury him in a cigar box," announced Kat.

"In a cigar box? You mean one of those cheap cardboard or wooden ones?" asked Denney.

"No, this is a nice burl wood with a gold inlay. She said the Colonel left it to us. I went ahead and told her she could have it. A cigar box sounds like another dead-end in our search for our inheritance anyway."

"Frankly, a cigar box, however nice, sounds insulting. I knew he didn't care for us but, that little? I'm not surprised, and it seems the only way our inheritance might show up is if we are sole survivors. Anyway, I'm going to speak with Vicar Dick about the arrangements for Petey."

By the way, Merriweather wants you to send out the notices to these select people, which includes Ashleigh. Also, I am thinking about a job as a preschool teacher. How hard can that be?"

Denney was pleased that Kat made it in time so as not to disturb her penchant for the ritual of evening Manhattans on the porch, but Petey's funeral was a lot of unexpected information, considering she had much to share herself.

Denney was unapologetic when she said, "You mean Peter, that freaky big, demented and neurotic parrot?" She knew Kat understood her comment as Kat often remarked that Petey *was* crazy after his traumatic experience with the greyhound. She didn't feel it necessary to talk about the funeral and instead launched into a detailed account of her research that revealed no other legitimate claims to the Colonel's estate other than their own.

"Kat, you know Winfield? Well, he walked into the library with some scruffy-looking guy."

"Once again, he is showing up where we are," Kat said anxiously. "I find that to be disturbing and worrisome! Or am I imagining it? Why would he come here? Could he be here to hurt Ashleigh, do you think? Is he following us to get to Ashleigh, or is he following us to get to us? Could this have anything to do with him being a cousin to the Colonel? But how could that be important? He has no claim to anything of ours or the Colonel. Don't 'cha think? Oh well, perhaps I should cut back on my Manhattans."

"My dear Kat," Denney said, peering over her cherry-red reading glasses, "I am intrigued you would blame your obvious paranoia on my Manhattans! On the other hand, you might be right. Recalling what dear departed Sigmund said, "In the depths of my heart, I can't help being convinced my fellow men, with few exceptions, are worthless.""

"Well shit," said Kat. "I suppose that is a relief." Kat downed her first Manhattan and poured herself a second, clinking glasses with Denney.

Chapter 21

Holy Wisdom!

The sisters got up early as there was a lot to do. It had taken the better part of the previous evening to get all but one drawer open on the desk. The top right-hand drawer was still stuck. As the sisters had their morning coffee with their breakfast bars, a lamp was warming the exterior of the obstinate drawer.

Denney was tired; she wasn't used to rising so early. "Kat, what do you think overall of the desk?"

"Well, in one way, it's a disappointment. It is a lovely, quirky piece of furniture, but it doesn't seem to fit into the overall search for the Colonel's remaining estate."

Denney offered, "I think we've spent a bit too much time and far too much emotional capital just to find a desk."

Both were so tired their eyes were glazing over.

"Well, let's check that last drawer before I ruin my nails trying to pry it open," sighed Denney.

"You're telling me you are still paying that exorbitant spa to get your nails done when I'm worried about paying the bills and becoming a pre-school teacher? I certainly won't be paying for your damn nails then!" Kat huffed.

"My dear, we'll just stop drinking your imported bottled water then and save it that way. There's plenty of bourbon in the pantry for sufficient hydration."

As they wiggled the drawer, they were both surprised to find the drawer opened more easily. Perhaps it was due to the loosening of the other drawers, or maybe they had weakened something. They considered both consequences and decided anything could be fixed.

As they coaxed out the drawer, there was something inside. Painstakingly, they pulled until they could grip both sides firmly with their fingertips and pull with a little more authority. Suddenly, the more swollen part of the drawer passed through the desk's face and opened fully.

Inside, something was wrapped in brown craft paper and tied with twine. Kat took it out carefully and laid it upon the top of the desk. As she reached for the razor blade to cut the twine, Denney whispered, "Stop."

"What?"

"Let's open it in the potting shed. There's no telling what could be in there."

She looked at her with some disbelief, "Oh, c'mon."

"Okay, let's take it to the kitchen," said Denney.

Inside the package was an old Polaroid picture of the Colonel with his coronet across his lap. He was flanked by a woman who was partially out of the picture and unrecognizable. He had on a pale linen suit. A Panama skimmer sat cocked on his head. The background was apparently a beautiful tropical home, with an arched walkway and a stunning motif of elephants and cobras.

"Look, the etched motif on the archway is the same as the details on the desk." Kat carefully rewrapped the picture to keep it from fading and placed it back in the same drawer for safekeeping.

"You know, if the desk and the picture are all this amounts to, then it's just another dead-end. First, the additional furniture in the carriage house that produced no clues, then the envelope with only the family tree information and now this, the desk with no real lead in it."

Kat was making her way upstairs to shower but paused on the stairway and addressed Denney, "I think you're right. I feel certain we'll be able to figure it out."

It was midday when the phone rang. Neither sister answered. Kat hated all the relentless telemarketing calls. She would let the caller leave a message if it was important and check it later. She came downstairs with her damp hair still wrapped in a towel. As she passed the answering machine, she decided to see if any of the calls that morning were important. After hearing one hang-up after another, she heard Ashleigh's voice. He sounded distraught and said he would be over at five o'clock p.m. and begged them to be home. Kat turned to Denney and asked her to listen to the message.

"Denney, is this going to interfere with our evening libations?" she asked after listening to the message. "I'm telling you that after the way things have been going, I don't want to miss that chance to unwind."

Bourbon & Benjamins

Still, Denney appeared concerned. "You know this is odd. As pushy as Ashleigh can be, he's never acted like this. I fear he may be in trouble, Kat."

"Well, shit."

"That seems to be your go-to response lately," replied Denney.

"No shit!"

It was 4:45 p.m., and Ashleigh was making his way up the sidewalk. They were waiting in their chairs on the front porch, and Kat had lugged a rather heavy plastic Adirondack chair up front for Ashleigh. Ashleigh hurried to the front porch, spied the available chair, and plopped down with a thud, as the chair was rather low-slung.

"Ashleigh, dear, you look ashen. What's wrong? You are not your bouncy self," said Denney.

Ashleigh was now thirsty and asked if he could have one of what the girls were drinking. Kat said, "Nope."

Denney felt bad and said, "Just kidding—but frankly, you look like you'd be better off with some cool water and lemon."

Ashleigh was okay with that, and Denney asked Kat, "Would you mind getting Ashleigh some water?"

"No," said Kat.

Denney, now peeved, got up and came back with a tall glass of iced water with lemon. Kat turned to Ashleigh and said, "I know your game; you would do anything to stay as long as you can, so you'd better spill whatever it is you have to say."

Ashleigh looked kind of guilty and said, "Let's let Denney sit, please."

Kat grudgingly acquiesced. Ashleigh said, "My brother, Winfield, is in town. He called me and asked to stay at my place. I didn't know what to say. Mother and Father warned me he was a bad seed, and I should never have anything to do with him. I felt so bad I acted like someone was at the door and said I'd call him back. He said, 'No, I'll call you in a few minutes.'"

"I hurriedly called Vicar Dick and asked his advice. He told me that under no circumstances was I to have anything to do with Winfield. I asked him how I could put him off. Vicar Dick said, 'Just say you have company this weekend.' I thought instead, and perhaps I could stay here."

Denney jumped in. "Ashleigh, if you weren't at home, there would be no reason for Winfield not to stay at your place. Instead, you need company. Not women, mind you, but a male friend. Hmm, how about Jeremy?"

"What if Jeremy says I don't have enough fans?"

Kat chimed in. "It doesn't matter; just use it as an excuse, and maybe Jeremy will come over."

He stood and thanked them for listening and excused himself. He ran home to call Jeremy.

They were relieved the visit was short. Nevertheless, Winfield being in town started to make sense and they were concerned for Ashleigh.

***

Winfield had also spoken with Beau Buford and was curious why Kat and Denney were tracking a desk that had been the Colonel's. In his mind, that was his too. Anything that belonged to the Colonel was his too, by right.

Winfield made a sharp turn to the left into the Motel Interstate. To get to Louisville, Asmond had used the money Winfield gave him in New Orleans.

When Winfield entered the motel room, he saw Asmond had an open bottle of rot-gut bourbon and a bag of Cheetos on a small table.

"Care to join me?" offered Asmond.

Winfield sized him up as if he were an insect under a microscope. Without emotion, he crisply declined the drink and said, "This won't take long." He looked again at Asmond and thought he had no interior life if he had to dwell in such a pestilential hole. For whatever else Winfield may have become, his private boarding school education taught him the value of vocabulary and specificity in language.

He adopted a superficial charm and said, "You know... you and I go way back."

Asmond belched and said, "Sure."

Winfield, knowing Asmond was just a mendicant and was always down on his luck, proposed a job that would pay a decent amount. Winfield felt his family's fortune would soon be his, and he could buy or sell a dozen Asmond's. He would dispose of him if he became a liability.

"Look, these two old dipsomaniac spinsters, that's drunk to you, have a peculiar desk that was supposed to be delivered to me," he lied, "and I need it back immediately. Some dipshit clerk sent it to them, and they're sitting on it. It's mine, and I want it."

Asmond's beady eyes were trained on Winfield, "So you want me to boost a desk?" as he stuffed his mouth with Cheetos and washed them down with more Kentucky Bourbon. "Why don't you just go get it if it's yours?"

Winfield realized that drinking bourbon that tasted like rotted raisins and rated generally at .5 out of 10 meant Asmond was ready for the job, but he bristled at Asmond's challenging tone.

"If you don't want the job, I can leave now!" Winfield scowled.

But Asmond asked, "What's in it for me? I want the job, but I gotta be paid. Some old desk ain't worth much, and what if there's trouble?"

Winfield looked at him with narrowing eyes and said, *"Like I said,* it's mine, and they stole it. I'm going to pay you, and you'll get a couple of months' rent out of it. That's all you need to know."

As Winfield glared at Asmond, he unleashed the poison in his mind. His parents, his dimwitted and worthless brother, and those conniving bitches had conspired to take away his inheritance and liberty and ruin his life. He was determined to get it all back.

He had learned to hate the Colonel. When he was an adolescent, he had so admired the man and wanted to be his son. Whenever the Colonel and Winfield's father got together to discuss business, Winfield was always lurking about and watching. When he returned from boarding school at eighteen years old, he would listen to every word the Colonel said.

Winfield practiced the older man's mannerisms behind closed doors in his room, in front of the full-length mirror just to get every physical movement and facial expression just right. His mother would say it was remarkable how closely he resembled the Colonel. He often daydreamed that the Colonel was his birth father at the boarding school, holding his biological father in contempt. He felt the Colonel would agree that he was the son he had always wished for. After all, Ashleigh, his twin brother, was nothing short of a buffoon and the Colonel never displayed any interest whatsoever in his twin.

The two daughters the Colonel produced by his wife were unimportant. They were girls, and girls meant nothing to men like himself and the Colonel. Others may have called him a boy because of his age, but he was cunning like a man and carried himself like one. A small contemptuous smile creased the corners of his mouth as he recalled his love for the Colonel and how he was rebuffed when the Colonel did not return his admiration and affection.

Once again, he strengthened his resolve to get it all back.

Winfield told Asmond the current location of the desk and gave him a picture of the sisters.

Asmond asked if Winfield had already had dinner. Winfield, not one to linger, declined Asmond's offer of Vienna sausages. Now short on patience and social graces and eager to leave, asked hurriedly, "You got it?" spat Winfield.

"This ain't my first boost, yeah, I got it," replied Asmond as he took another swig of the Kentucky Bourbon.

***

Back at St. James Court, Kat and Denney decided to retire for the evening. They had completed the evening ritual and were relieved to know Ashleigh was not the one skulking around. Certain that it was Winfield, they were now on guard because he was in town and by all accounts, crazy.

"Well, you can't mistake Ashleigh or Winfield for anyone else, that's for sure!" offered Kat as she and Denney climbed the stairs for bed.

"And, unless Ashleigh starts wearing Ferragamo's, the two are quite distinguishable," added Denney. "I guess I'm relieved that poor Ashleigh didn't have a break with reality and develop two personas."

Kat agreed. "Holy wisdom!" She sighed with relief.

Chapter 22

Oh Petey, Oh Petey

Uncharacteristically, Denney was the first to wake. She decided something different would be nice to accompany their breakfast bars. She was going to make smoothies, but they were out of kale. As she bustled about the kitchen, Kat joined her.

"Crikey! What has you up so early?" Kat mused as she rubbed her eyes.

"I couldn't sleep thinking about the funeral and all we have to do this morning." Denney was somewhat OCD. It didn't show up in everything she did, but when it did raise its peculiar head, Denney was absorbed.

"I think we should have some yogurt and honey with our breakfast bars this morning. I have that delightful new honey from the local beekeeper," Denney said lightly.

"I've got the coffee!" said Kat. As the coffee steeped in the French press, she admired her new frothier. "Yogurt sounds good *and* fast. We do have a full morning."

The sisters finished their morning routine and walked to Mrs. Merriweather's. They wanted to supervise the delivery of the flowers and set up the parlor for Petey's funeral. The only dog that accompanied them today was Rusty, as requested by Mrs. Merriweather. She held the notion that Rusty and Petey were friends. But Kat knew otherwise. Rusty usually ignored Petey and came to Merriweather's for the little creamers she shared with him and to be with Kat.

As they approached Merriweather's house, Rusty became more excited. Pulling at his leash, he broke free and scurried to her front door. There he waited patiently for Kat to catch up. Kat, walking arm and arm with Denney, exclaimed, "How do you think he is going to take the death of Petey?"

Denney was well-acquainted with Petey's history. "Unless he has a coffee creamer strapped to his huge, feathery chest, he won't even notice."

Rusty wiggled as they approached and started pawing at the front door.

They heard Mrs. Merriweather shout, "I'm coming," in her high-pitched, twittery voice.

Rusty bolted into the parlor as soon as she opened the door wide enough. He curiously looked around. Then nearing the coffee table, he began looking for the coffee creamers. "Oh, poor baby, I forgot all about your coffee creamers," she cooed to Rusty. "You know, Petey is gone now, Rusty, and in my grief, I forgot to get them."

Rusty dipped his head and looked stricken as only a brown-eyed cocker spaniel could do.

Kat turned to Denney and said, "You generally have everything in your purse. Do you have a creamer in there?"

Denney reached the bottom corner of her purse and retrieved a gnarly French vanilla creamer. She had taken it with her from Bob Evans a week ago and offered it up.

Rusty had been sitting patiently, but now his butt wiggled in anticipation. He immediately lay down by the coffee table, his regular spot, placed the creamer between his front paws, and starting to slurp out the contents.

"Have a seat, dears, while I get the coffee," Merriweather offered in her same sweet voice.

Over coffee, they discussed preparing the parlor. Denney looked at Kat with wide eyes and then down at her coffee cup. Kat gave a knowing smile. The coffee was more rum than bean.

As they decided where the table with the humidor would be placed, the doorbell rang. It was the florist with all the arrangements. Tears came to Merriweather's eyes as the delivery man brought in each floral piece.

Merriweather's tone had turned pensive now. She sighed and said, "Denney, they are just beautiful. You girls go ahead and set things up as I finish my coffee."

Kat and Denney finished their second cup of coffee as the final arrangement was put in place. In twenty minutes, the guests would arrive, and it was time to freshen up.

Denney rushed to the powder room. "I'll just be a minute. You know I can't allow my lipstick to wear off in public," she said lightly.

"Don't take too long in that bathroom," Kat shouted back, "I just had my teeth whitened professionally, and coffee stains might mess 'em up. I'm not taking any chances."

Mrs. Merriweather had somewhat composed herself and decided to make more coffee, laced amply, for them and her guests. As Denney came out of the powder room, the aromatic vapors of fresh coffee enticed her to have a third cup.

Kat followed and said, "Fix me one of those too."

Cup in hand, Kat greeted the several guests arriving on time. Vicar Dick arrived first and moved quickly to Denney to discuss his eulogy. Ashleigh was hot on Vicar Dick's heels. He was damp as usual, so Kat seated him in front of the window air-conditioner despite his overuse of Jade East cologne.

Hulda Meisterman arrived shortly after that, with Mildred Purvis practically overtaking her. Kat ignored their antics, although she knew that their rivalry was boundless, even to the point of who arrived first at any church-related event. "Please join us for coffee before the service," offered Kat as she greeted each guest at the front door.

A few of Merriweather's neighbors and Winky Danville, the longtime rival of Denney, came last. Winky brought a box of her homemade caramels. Merriweather handed each person a china teacup and saucer as they entered the parlor. It was a sacred part of the ceremony.

Denney saw Winky entering and getting her coffee, and right away, she could feel the tension in her shoulders tighten. Winky would light up like a Christmas tree when anyone bit into one of her caramels. It was obvious she loved the attention. Winky made sure she offered one to all the guests. Vicar Dick took one bite and praised her for her gift of candy-making.

"It really goes well with this coffee. I think I have time for one more and coffee, too," the vicar replied.

Winky blushed with pleasure and gave him another caramel while Merriweather, who was now manning the coffee station, refilled his coffee cup.

Denney signaled to Vicar Dick he could begin the service. Since the Vicar had not had much contact with Petey, she had assisted him in preparing his eulogy. He was grateful for the help and focused his remarks on Merriweather's loving relationship with Petey and how everyone benefitted from the companionship of a dear pet. Then he asked Ms. Merriweather to come forward and deliver her remarks.

Ms. Merriweather slowly walked forward and faced her friends. With a slight quiver in her voice, she said, "I would like to share a poem I wrote for my dear Petey." With that, she began.

"Oh Petey, Oh Petey

My feathered best friend

How much I do miss you

And will to the end."

Merriweather sighed and paused before returning to her notes.

"Your beautiful plumage

And sweet spoken words

Always delighted

Like the sweetest songbird."

At this, Merriweather dabbed at her eyes with her handkerchief.

Kat approached her with a small glass of water.

Merriweather waved her away, saying, "I'm fine, dear.

Now in bird heaven

I lay you to rest

My sad concession

As you were the best."

There was a moment of silence as Merriweather took her seat and the vicar walked to the front of the room.

Kat had directed Vicar Dick to close the service with a prayer from the *Book of Common Prayer* and had selected the one on page 840 titled "Thanksgiving for the Beauty of the Earth." The vicar was to insert, after the words "for the songs of birds," the additional "and the song of Petey." However, the vicar and the rest of the guests had at a minimum two cups of Mrs. Merriweather's strong, rum-laced coffee. Now ready to close the service, the vicar reached for his prayer book. Instead of turning to page 840 in the *Book of Common Prayer*, he clumsily turned to page

820. He began reading the prayer for the President of the United States and all in authority. Nobody noticed but Kat and Denney. Merriweather was snoring lightly on the couch, and Hulda Meisterman was annoyed with Rusty, who now had turned on his back, exposing himself after finishing Mildred's cup of coffee.

Kat covered her mouth to stifle a laugh. She looked at Denney, who hung her head to hide her amusement. Kat moved closer to Ashleigh, who already had two cups of coffee to fight the chill, when he announced, in sotto voce, "Can I get an Amen?"

As if on cue, Rusty woke up and padded to the front door. Following suit, the guests turned to Mrs. Merriweather and expressed their condolences to her half-sleeping figure.

Kat turned to Denney. "We need to clean up the dishes and let's leave a note for Merriweather to let her know we're taking Petey with us. I'll also add we're going to bury him in the garden and that the service was beautiful." The humidor was tucked securely under Kat's arm. Rusty walked alongside Denney with his leash dragging behind him.

***

Asmond had taken up surveillance during the funeral near the St. James Court fountain. He had a tourist map of Old Louisville opened and dangling from his hand. He decided it gave him a cover.

Asmond knew he owed Winfield for helping him escape from prison, and he had no problem being the muscle and not the brains. At best, his intellect was patchy, but he knew Winfield's money would be good and Asmond always needed money. He made his way around the fountain and saw a black and white party cocker walking behind two women. The dog was trailing his leash on the sidewalk, and the women looked familiar. He pulled out the photo and looked it over carefully. Yes, the women looked strikingly like the two in the photo. He decided to follow them at a careful distance. Perhaps his luck might change, and he could wrap this up quickly.

Asmond watched as Kat and Denney entered their house. He stopped on the sidewalk and looked at the house carefully.

Margie Dumeyer, their next-door neighbor, was raking some leaves from under her shrubbery. She looked at Asmond, and squinting into the setting sun, asked, "May I help you?"

Asmond had switched to what he thought was his charming persona so as not to alarm her. He was now clean-shaven and dressed in respectable khaki pants, a pale blue golf shirt, and a pair of polished brown loafers. "Oh, that's quite all right. I'm from out of town, an architect, and I am just marveling at the well-maintained Victorian here."

"Oh my, yes," twittered Mrs. Dumeyer. "You're looking at one of the nicest examples, but you should really look at the next block too, just stunning."

"Thank you so much," said Asmond. "If you don't mind, I'd love to see your turret a little more closely. It won't take but a minute or two."

"Sure, don't mind me, just tidying up," she said, suddenly feeling less at ease, and looked at him carefully because now he was becoming more intrusive. Since he looked like a tourist, she dismissed her foreboding.

Asmond walked toward the curved turret on the front of Margie's house and, when he was out of her direct sight, turned to get a better look at the front porch and door of Kat and Denney's home. The front door was recessed enough that a person standing there would not be easily seen by either neighbor. The windows looked newer and solid.

He walked back to the sidewalk, thanked Margie, and said, "As you suggested, I'll certainly check out the architecture in the next block."

Feeling better, Margie smiled as if she had just talked to a potential suitor. "You're mighty welcome."

Asmond walked to the corner and looked back. Margie had stopped her clean-up and was no longer in front of the house. Asmond had finished his first reconnaissance.

***

Kat and Denney, who had arrived home feeling hungry, set the humidor on top of the island counter in the kitchen while Denney made sandwiches of watercress and cream cheese on sprouted wheat bread. Rusty joined Jules and Gus outside on the deck to enjoy the cooler evening shade.

Kat turned to Denney and said, "How about something different with our sandwiches, say a vodka and tonic?"

Denney, who fought any change to her routine, felt magnanimous after the success of the funeral and halfheartedly said, "Sure."

Kat happily headed for the limes, vodka, and tonic. "Denney, would you get the crushed ice and take our sandwiches to the rear deck? You can assess the backyard for a suitable place to inter Petey."

Denney felt she was back in charge. "Of course, you know I have a sharp eye for symmetry. I think the brick path leading to the bower with the trailing wisteria espalier would be a fitting place for Petey to rest. You know, under the wisteria. It looks like it will have one of its best years. It will be like a piece of heaven." said Denney.

"Those large lavender blooms are smashing," agreed Kat.

The sisters finished their sandwiches, and Denney cleared the plates and glasses.

"I'm going to the potting shed to get my gloves and garden spade," said Kat.

Kat opened the potting shed while the dogs were still resting quietly on the deck. She walked down the brick path, putting on her garden gloves while the garden spade was tucked under one arm.

She waited for Denney to pick up the humidor to join her in front of the espalier. As Kat started gently clearing the area of rich, black topsoil digging Petey's final resting place,

Rusty raised his head, his nose started twitching and he started toward the burial site. Kat paused her digging. Denney had arrived and opened the humidor one last time to see that all was intact.

Denney noticed that the velvet cover under Petey had shifted, exposing the corner of what appeared to be an envelope. She grabbed Petey and tossed him aside. "Kat! Look! What the freakin'..." Her voice trailed off.

In the meantime, Rusty gently picked up Petey and took him back to the deck. Kat saw Rusty with feathers sticking out of his mouth and screamed, "What the fuck!"

"Shocked, Denney said, "I know! This is an envelope."

Kat turned and yelled, "For shit's sake, Denney, Rusty has Petey!"

Denny turned and saw Rusty, "Drop it, damn it." Denney ordered in a very deep and controlled voice.

Rusty complied. He spat out Petey and just sat behind the ruffled and slobbery parrot.

Kat could now turn to Denney and look into the humidor. "Pull it out, Denney! Just pull the damn thing out."

Denney pulled the velvet covering aside and the thin cardboard underneath it and snatched the envelope. "It's empty."

"It probably wasn't because the cardboard under the blanket is mounded as if something much fatter were stuffed below it. Petey was just holding it down. Tomorrow we are going back to see Merriweather!"

Kat retrieved Petey from the yard and smoothed him out as best she could, commanding Rusty to STAY. Denney replaced the cardboard liner and velvet blanket in the humidor, and Kat placed Petey in the center and shut the lid.

Kat dug the hole a little deeper, her spade hitting rock. At that, she moved a little forward and began digging again. She hit what she thought was metal, and it was a tinny, hollow sound, unlike hitting a rock or brick. Kat said to Denney, "Before we go any further, I think a Manhattan is in order, as I just hit something metal. I'll wait here while you fix 'em."

Consumed with curiosity, Kat knelt and started uncovering the lid of a small tin box with her gloved hands. Taking off her gloves, she could wiggle the box and, digging her fingers underneath, pried it loose. She set it beside her on the grass, next to the humidor.

Denney was approaching with two glasses when she saw the box on the ground. "SHUUUT UUUPP! Is that what was there?"

Kat grabbed the box and said, "Follow me!"

Denney turned on her heel, glasses in hand, and rushed to follow Kat inside. She watched her as she searched through the cutlery drawer. "Just pull out a steak knife."

Kat pulled out a steak knife and began prying open the rusty lid. It popped open, exposing a rusty keyring with five keys.

Denney pulled out the keys. "I can't make any sense of this. Do you think we should also ask Merriweather about this tomorrow? Since she had the Colonel's cigar box, maybe she could shed some light on this too."

"No," responded Kat. "Let's sit on this for a while. We'll put these in the desk for now."

"Yes, it has been a long day, what with the funeral and all," Denney agreed.

Kat's eyes got big, and she gasped, "Petey!"

It was now dark, and Petey's humidor was covered in dew.

"We have to get that little dickens in the ground," gasped Denney.

"Merriweather would never forgive us," agreed Kat.

They made their way back to Petey and placed him in his grave. Denney put the first spade of earth over his coffin, and Kat finished. Rusty ambled toward them, and when all three were in front of the grave, Kat offered a simple prayer and placed a flat rock over the site.

They all returned to the house without a sound and settled in for the night.

Chapter 23

I'll Have What She's Having

It was a long but pleasant mid-afternoon walk to Merriweather's, as the sun was not too hot and the sidewalk was shaded. They decided to walk for some exercise and didn't want to bring Rusty this time, as he had his own agenda when walking, and carrying him was not an option.

Merriweather's cottage was on what was referred to as a walking court. There was a generous sidewalk running between facing cottages. When they arrived at Merriweather's, they drew a deep breath and knocked at the door.

Mrs. Merriweather answered the door and, seeing them, spontaneously declared, "I loved that bird to the end! Where did you bury him?" Her tone was a bit challenging as they suspected she might be miffed at not having been there.

Kat responded, "Merriweather, pull yourself together. Remember, we talked about this and agreed we would bury him. Your backyard is small, and you said you didn't want to leave him there after you were gone. We put him under the espalier. His burial was quite lovely and done with dignity."

Mrs. Merriweather was still standing in the doorframe and had not moved to invite them in.

"Which brings us to another matter," Denney said while moving closer into Mrs. Merriweather's personal space and practically compelling her to step back and let them in.

Merriweather collected herself and retreated to her usual greeting, "Would you like a cup of coffee?"

Without hesitation, Kat irritably exclaimed, "No!" When the coffee started flowing, she knew that Mrs. Merriweather would lose her concentration, and they would play hell getting her to circle back.

Mrs. Merriweather appeared a little taken aback but sat dutifully in her armchair. Kat approached her and took her hands, and said, "Okay, dear, we need to talk with you about something extremely important."

Denney was overly agitated at this point. She bumped Kat aside. "I have skipped my second cup of coffee this morning to attend services and still beat the hotter part of the day. I've had enough. In Petey's humidor, it seemed there might have been other stuff tucked away under the cardboard liner." She stared intently at Merriweather. "Before you placed the velvet blanket in the humidor, did you see something like that?"

"What?" Mrs. Merriweather looked blankly at Denney.

Denney, more vexed, said, "I took great pains to word my question explicitly."

Kat bumped Denney out of the way and said, "Merriweather, there was some other shit in that humidor besides the bird. Now go get it."

Mrs. Merriweather turned and looked at Kat and said, "Oh, yes, dear, I know exactly what you're talking about. I saved it for you girls. Let me see… I need to think about where I put it. Can I get you a cup of coffee while you wait?"

Kat looked at Denney, and they realized it was inevitable they would share some coffee this morning.

Kat exhaled and replied, "Sure." She watched Merriweather bustle off to the kitchen and decided to follow her to see if she could speed up her memory a bit.

Mrs. Merriweather opened the cabinet to pull out a coffee filter, and Kat saw a large manilla envelope resting on top of the filters. Merriweather moved the envelope aside and retrieved a coffee filter, and she began to close the cabinet door.

"Wait! What is that envelope you just moved?" Kat shouted.

"What envelope, dear?" replied Merriweather.

Kat pointed to the envelope and said, "Dang it, Merriweather, THAT envelope," pointing into the cabinet.

Mrs. Merriweather reached for the envelope and said, "Where did this come from. Did you put this up here?"

Denney was squirming. She got up and went to the kitchen. The first thing she noticed was Kat with an envelope. *Praise be!* she thought.

"Kat," Denney said, "is that THE envelope?"

"I certainly hope so; let's have a cup of coffee and peek into it before going home."

Denney said, "Kat, please take my coffee into the parlor," as she snatched the envelope from her. "I'll just be a moment," and she ran to the bathroom.

Kat heard a high-pitched squeal of delight coming from the small washroom.

Merriweather looked at Kat and said, "I trust she is all right."

Kat assured her all was okay. She added, "Do you remember that line from the movie, 'I'll have what she's having?' Well, it's sorta like that."

Merriweather mumbled, "No, I don't recall it."

Denney emerged from the washroom looking radiant.

They both turned and looked at her. Merriweather slapped her hand over her mouth and, in a whisper, said, "Oh, *okay*, I remember now."

Denney sat down on the couch with the envelope firmly clasped on her lap as they each drank half of their coffee and started their goodbyes.

Merriweather was calm now and escorted them to the door. "It's always good to see you; it's been too long, dears."

Kat gave Mrs. Merriweather a quick hug and said, "See ya soon."

They started a fast-paced walk home. Denney was struggling to keep pace but wanted to get there as quickly as possible, too.

Kat kept questioning her about the contents of the envelope. Denney, hot and irritated now, snapped, "Do you want me to tell you in the ambulance or when we get home?"

Kat looked at Denney with a bit of worried concern, recalling the time Denney responded to high stress on the golf course and didn't want to add that to the excitement around the envelope's content. So, she kept quiet until they got home, keeping a watchful eye on her.

Once at home, they went to the kitchen and solemnly placed the envelope on the table. Like a spiritual moment, that very instant the sun rounded the side of the house and shone through the kitchen window, vibrantly lighting the room. Kat lifted the envelope and inverted it ever so carefully. Out tumbled a pile of folded and beribboned documents.

Denney, who had already picked around inside the envelope said in a hushed tone, "Look at them closely, Kat."

Kat selected the top document, untied the ribbon, unfolded the document, and shrieked, "Jesus, Joseph, and Mary! Are the rest like this?"

Denney smiled, leaned back in her chair, and nodded

her head affirmatively. "Yes, there are deeds, stock certificates, and certificates of deposit."

Kat asked, "Could there be—I'm thinking—millions of dollars here?"

Before thinking logically and engaging her legal background, Denney participated in the moment and exclaimed, "Well, hell yeah!"

Kat became serious. "We need to safeguard these, and let's not go talking about them—just tuck them away for now."

The sisters did not have a floor safe, and their tiny fireproof box was already crammed full.

Denney looked around and saw the desk. "Let's put them in the desk for now, and maybe this will get us motivated to buy a real safe tomorrow."

Dusk was approaching and they decided to relax.

"Life is back on track, don't you think?" asked Denney. "We can sustain ourselves for sure. Not that I was ever worried."

Kat had prepared the Manhattans more potent than usual. "I guess I shouldn't have worried so much, but I need our elixir tonight for sure. It has been challenging!"

Denney dusted off the cushions on the wicker chairs and the dogs started to assemble on the front porch. It was as if nothing special had happened. It was certainly just another day in their lives to any onlooker.

Chapter 24

Damn it, It Never Fails

Kat was up first to let the dogs out for their morning run. She went back into the foyer and yelled up the staircase to Denney, "Are you up? Come on down and let's take our breakfast on the back porch and celebrate our good fortune.

Denney shouted back, "Go on out, I'll be there in a minute."

***

Asmond was lurking across the street, watching the house. He lit a cigarette and muttered, "When are they going to leave the house?" He flicked his lit cigarette to the ground, crushing it with the toe of his shoe and pausing to make sure no one was out front raking leaves or walking dogs or any of several pedestrian activities common to the outside. The ground was damp as he crossed the green space. He walked up to the sisters' front door, leaving wet footprints in his wake. The screen door was unlocked, and it opened easily, but the wooden door was locked. He gently tried the doorknob a couple of times to be sure. He walked around to the side of the house, almost to the rear corner and heard talking. He hesitated and waited.

***

Kat had walked to the wisteria-covered bower espalier and waited for Denney. As she checked Petey's grave, Denney made her way to Kat and they both looked at Petey's resting place.

"It all looks good to me, and nothing is disturbed. Let's go back to the porch and have our coffee and Baileys," said Kat.

Suddenly, Gus started barking. There were no squirrels, birds, or chipmunks around. "Well, Gus, there's nothing to bark about. Be quiet."

***

Asmond was startled. He looked around to see if the dog's barking had stirred anyone. As the dogs settled down, he took a breath. He could still hear the sisters talking. He continued to wait patiently, out of sight. He knew he couldn't steal the desk unless they left, and he was looking for a different opportunity. Denney and Kat were so much more relaxed now that they had a link to their inheritance and no longer had such fear of an ignominious end.

Kat looked at Denney and asked, "Seriously, how much do you think is there?'

Denney looked at her gravely and said, "Honestly, until we find these pieces of property we won't know for sure, but I have got to imagine, due to the mere acreage we are looking at hundreds of thousands of dollars, not to mention the other documents. But we don't know what's on the property. It could be developed, or it could be a wasteland."

Gus, who had been lying at Denney's feet, raised his head, sniffed, and started to bark again.

***

Asmond had overheard the last of their conversation. His mind was racing. What did Winfield want with some old desk? Either or both of these old broads could be ransomed for a lot more. The property alone could be sold and bring a pretty penny. But maybe Winfield knew that, and he would use this heist to frame him for something bigger. His mind ran through a dozen possible scenarios in record time. He'd been double-crossed before. Didn't he learn anything from taking those falls?

Dismissing the fact that Winfield had made his escape possible, Asmond turned slightly to his right to look through the corner window. He could see a desk sitting in the foyer. Obviously, it hadn't found a place yet. That had to be the desk that was just delivered. It was an odd, bulky piece, and he could never move it without someone knowing. That made him even more sure Winfield was setting him up. He decided to call him and tell him he had found the desk and that he should come himself to claim it.

Asmond pulled out the burner Winfield had given him and dialed.

Winfield answered quickly. "What?!" he growled.

"Look, have you ever seen this desk? It's an ugly,

bulky piece of junk," Asmond loudly whispered. "You need to come up with another plan. In fact, you need to come and just claim it."

"Look Ass-mond, why do I have to come? That wasn't the deal," Winfield hissed.

Asmond continued in his frantic whisper. "I was listening around the corner of their place, and I heard those broads say that Goodwill was going to pick it up in the morning. Besides, it looks like they ain't goin' nowhere tonight."

Winfield was clearly annoyed. "Shit, Asmond. I can't get there until nine tonight. I'll have to meet you." He told Asmond he would meet him on the corner of 4th and Park at nine o'clock that evening and hung up abruptly, not saying what would happen then.

Asmond had no intention of doing that. He spent the afternoon developing his ruse to lure Winfield to the house after he had disposed of one sister and kidnapped the other. When Winfield arrived at the corner, he would call him and tell him he needed to be at the house, and he would have the door open. Then he would implicate Winfield by calling 911 and reporting a domestic in progress. Winfield would be standing in the middle of a homicide.

Meanwhile, Asmond would be as far away as possible, attempting to demand a large sum of money from the sister he kidnapped in return for her release. It wasn't entirely worked out in his mind, but he thought he was smart enough to ad-lib it. It was almost dark.

***

Kat and Denney finished their cocktails and walked inside. It was almost 8:15 p.m. Gus followed, but Rusty and Jules had sniffed out something more interesting in the backyard. Nothing was disturbed, nothing was wrong, and Gus was now calm. Denney petted Gus and said, "Come on upstairs with me, it's okay. You know how those other two fur-babies like to smoke out a chipmunk or two."

"I'm going to watch some TV, but first, why don't you help me move this desk out of the foyer and into the living room? Kat asked.

"Sure, but then I'm just going to change into something more comfortable. Where do you want it to go?"

"Maybe we could rearrange a few pieces tomorrow. We can just leave it out of the way for tonight," said Kat. They moved the bulky desk inside the parlor and close to the inside wall.

"Suits me," agreed Denney, then she went upstairs, entered her room, and put on her most comfortable pajamas.

Kat brewed some chamomile tea, settled into her favorite chair, put her feet up on the ottoman, and browsed through Netflix. She was going through the listings on their new smart TV when there was a knock on the door.

"Damn it, it never fails!" She got up and went to the door. "Yes?" she said through the closed door. She was already bemoaning the fact she had decided not to install the new doorbell and camera system, so she could have handled this without getting up.

"Yes, ma'am. A Mr. Ashleigh Daggit asked if I would come by and take a picture of the desk for him. I sure do apologize for stopping by after dinner, but he just called me," said Asmond.

Kat felt a chill go up her spine. This was so odd. "I don't know anything about this," said Kat, "and Ashleigh was just here... earlier."

Asmond didn't know what to say except, "I'm sorry, I can't really understand you."

Kat put the chain on the door and opened it slightly. "I said, I don't know what you are talking about. You'll have to get back to me tomorrow with Ashleigh."

With that, Asmond turned sideways and pushed the door in, pulling the old chain off the door frame.

Kat retreated and Asmond came in, closing the door behind him. He had a small automatic pistol in his right hand.

Denney, who had washed her face and applied a bright green cucumber paste as a toning mask, heard the commotion. She was about to call down the steps to Kat when she heard a gruff man's voice. "Where's the other broad who lives here?"

Kat was frozen. Asmond repeated himself, only louder and with a grizzled gruffness that was a lot more menacing.

Denney could feel the blood draining from her face under the green mask. *This is a home invasion*, she thought! She quickly pulled on her fluffy chenille robe and put her Ruger .380 in its generous pocket. It was fully loaded with jacketed hollow points. She left the robe untied so the folds of the cloth would hide any bulges at her side. She was at the top of the stairs now but not in sight.

Gus went barreling down the steps barking like mad. Rusty and Jules were still outside and started barking too when they heard Gus.

Asmond was distracted for a second. "Get that stupid four-legged rat outta' here."

Kat eyed Asmond, and asked him defiantly, "Who are you? What do you want?" as she turned to put Gus outside through the kitchen door.

"Just shut up and keep walking," he growled. Kat headed through the kitchen and to the back door.

As Denney quietly went down the stairs, she called 911. She touched the side of her robe and felt the solid outline of the Ruger. Her heart raced at the thought that she had a chance to show her skill and defend her home.

The operator answered. "What is your emergency?"

"It's a home invasion. My home." The operator asked for the address and Denney told her as quickly as she could.

"Can you stay on the phone? A unit is being dispatched now."

"I don't know," whispered Denney.

Then the back door shut and the man shouted, "Okay, where is she?"

Kat replied, "What?"

Asmond held up his gun and menacingly pointed at her head. Kat managed to croak as loudly as possible, "Don't shoot! We were outside, and she said she was going to the potting shed. I imagine with the dogs carrying on she will be back any minute. Why don't you leave while you still can?"

At that moment, Denney whispered into the phone, "He has a gun!" She laid her phone on the console and took her gun out of her pocket.

"Wouldn't that be dandy?" snarled Asmond. He paused, "I guess I'll have to get rid of you and just take her, then."

Kat knew she had better stall, if only for a minute. "What do you want? What are you after?"

Asmond looked around. He couldn't shoot her and risk the other sister running. "You need to get that other broad in here and don't try anything."

Hearing this conversation, Denney gave a quick practice run, siting the gun at the fireplace mantel. She stood with her feet slightly apart, knees bent, and arms comfortably bent but straight forward. Then, so as not to lose her form, she crab-walked two feet, stepping slightly into the doorframe of the kitchen, her gun held high and aimed. She made sure her grip was as instructed and had Asmond in her gun site. The right side of her body was visible. To her left was the doorframe, the wall, and a cupboard in front of it.

Kat looked past Asmond at Denney and as Asmond turned his head to see where Kat was looking, Kat tried to motion to Denney to run. Denney stood less than twenty feet behind him, with a gun aimed right at his center mass.

Seeing Denney's gun, Kat immediately thought Denney was much better at this than her Junior Sailing skills. She also thought that Winky Danville would crap her pants when she heard about this one.

As Asmond turned, he saw Denney and then fired a quick shot. The bullet skimmed the cupboard and lodged in the wall, no more than two inches from the door frame. Asmond instinctively took a couple of steps back as if to gain a better vantage point. He was now facing the hall doorway.

Kat dove to floor behind the kitchen island.

The last thing on Denney's mind was squeeze, don't pull. The trigger on the Ruger had what she called "slack." She needed to take it up before squeezing. She squeezed the trigger of her loaded Ruger and it kicked. She hit Asmond's left shoulder and he fell to the ground on one knee. Denney slid to the left to avoid being hit.

He fired again and the bullet strayed, entering the living room.

Denney regained her grip and looked around the doorframe. Asmond was trying to get to his feet. He looked up and saw Denney. He couldn't push or pull himself up with his left arm. Apparently, his knees weren't as supple as perhaps they once were, but he raised his right arm and aimed in Denney's direction. His unsupported right hand sent two wildly errant shots into the air.

Denney never stopped aiming at Asmond. As he rose to stand, she moved a small step to the right to better shoot around the door frame. Her next five rounds were fast—and fatal. Asmond fell backwards, his gun resting on his open fingers. Three shots hit him center mass—that was enough.

Kat ran to Denney from behind the end of the breakfast island and grabbed her.

Denney was screaming the f-bomb as sweat ran down her cheeks, etching rivulets in her green mask. They both fell on their wobbling knees. Denney, realizing her enraged panic, thought, *Wow, there really is an appropriate time to say FUCK out loud.*

Just then, the front door burst open. In rushed three armed police officers. The first to enter yelled at Denney to put down her weapon, and she instantly complied and dropped her Ruger.

Outside, three patrol cars sat with their bright blue lights flashing as another pulled up.

***

Winfield rounded the corner from 4th Street onto Park Avenue at the Central Park entrance. Seeing all the police cars, he slowed, parked against the curb, and turned off his lights, then sat perfectly still.

***

After their statements had been given, the crime scene was documented, and the coroner removed Asmond's body.

It was late at night, and Margie and various neighbors had congregated out front. "I was so stunned when I heard the description of that awful intruder," Margie said. "It could have been me in this awful mess." Although Margie had seen Asmond as a potential suitor, she was now dismissive of him. "He talked to me, you know, I and I just *knew* he was a skunk."

Denney looked at the last officer on the scene and with puffy eyes and a very tired voice, "Do we have to stay here tonight or tomorrow night?"

The officer looked at both Kat and Denney and became sympathetic. He said, "No, just keep your cell phones with you and don't leave the county."

They moved the dogs to the unused workout room in the basement, left food and water and then hurriedly packed an overnight bag.

Chapter 25

What About Those Keys

The sisters woke the next morning at a Hilton Garden Inn. Denney was still sleepy. "How did we end up here?"

"It was the first place that came to mind. I wasn't thinking options." Kat said while starting to dress.

"Where are you going, Kat?"

"I've got to check on the house and let the dogs out. We must check the desk, too!" she said excitedly.

Denney moaned wearily, "Wait for me, we'll both go. You shouldn't have to enter that horrible crime scene by yourself."

Denney slumped in her seat in the Mark V as if she couldn't move as Kat drove home.

Kat was worried about the dogs. They had been alone for six hours. As she pulled up in front of the house, she said, "Denney, the dogs! I'm going to check on them. I'll meet you inside."

The fur-babies, as Kat and Denney called them, were very ready to go outside. As Kat opened the door to the workout room, all three sped past her up the steps to the kitchen and to the kitchen door as fast as they could.

Kat screamed, "Not that way, come here!" but it was too late.

Denney had entered the house just in time to see twelve paws speed through a sticky mess of Asmond's blood. Denney screamed the f-word about five times—in her mind, of course. She scrambled around the mess and ran outside to the garden hose.

"All of you! Get over here! Now!" ordered Denney. Luckily, the grass had absorbed some of the sticky goo, but Denney still turned her head as she grabbed each dog's leg and sprayed their sticky paws. After she had washed all twelve paws, she reentered the kitchen, leaving the fur-babies outside.

Kat was already on the phone calling clean-up and restoration firms. "When can you be here?" she said as Denney entered the room. "Today, I need you today! No, in the morning is too damn late to even contemplate. It's a crime scene!" she shouted frantically. "What do you mean you don't... Well, who does? Yes, it's been cleared by the police."

Denney decided that dealing with bloody paws was a better deal than hiring a clean-up crew.

Kat hung up and immediately started dialing the number she had found on the web. "Yes, hello! Yes, I need a crime scene clean-up. Yes, the police have cleared it. If I were the Mafia, I'd have my own fucking clean-up crew. Okay, when can you be here? Tomorrow? What the hell, can't you come today? Yeah, I'll pay a premium for after five o'clock." Kat gave them the address and her cell number and ended the call.

Denney had gone into the living room to check the desk. All was just as they left it. But she could still hear Kat's conversation. "Did they say they couldn't come until tomorrow?

"Yeah, but they'll come today."

"What did they think we are? Animals?"

"Don't get your panties in a wad. I took care of it," Kat responded.

Denney huffed. "Okay, join me in the living room," All the bullets had been removed from the plaster walls and there were tape marks indicating the evidence that had been retrieved by the police.

"I guess it will be a while before everything is back to normal," Kat said.

"I think things will never be quite the same," said Denney. "But this could be the start of a new normal, I guess."

They both sighed at the same time as they looked around the room. There was a long silence.

"Kat, this is too much. I'm going out to the garden."

Kat looked at the mess around her and went down to the basement to find the dog gates. She brought them up, cordoned off the kitchen, then locked the door behind her, and walked to the garden where Denney was standing.

"Denney, the kitchen is now off-limits. Use the cellar

door or the front door until the cleaners leave. We'll be taking all our meals out for a while. Cleaned or not, I just don't think I can eat in that room for a while.

Denney wasn't thinking food. Having surveyed the damage, she eyed Kat and lamented, "My plaster!"

The sisters decided to sit outside and enjoy the unspoiled backyard.

Later, Kat prepared the Manhattans, Denney dusted off the cushions on the wicker chairs, and the dogs assembled on the front porch. The front door frame had been repaired that morning. The new door locks would have to wait, but a couple of nails offered a bit more security. Kat was determined to get a security system that linked the doorbell, locks, and a video camera to an inside monitor. She checked the desk again and assured herself everything was safe. She also promised herself she would purchase a safe in the morning.

As Kat brought the tray to the front porch, the clean-up crew arrived. She escorted them inside through the back door and returned to the porch. She was careful not to trip over the resting dogs. Some cheese and water crackers were tastefully arranged on a china plate. The Manhattans were in martini glasses tonight.

Kat collapsed on the plush cushions in her chair. "Perhaps we can put this year behind us and move on," she said.

Tickled, Denney couldn't help herself as she looked at Kat and said, "I suppose you'll have to find something else to worry about, dear."

Kat turned to Denney and asked, "Well, what about those keys?"

Epilogue

Winfield started his car and slowly pulled out into the quiet street. He thought about his failure to acquire the desk and his diminished hope of acquiring his inheritance. He was furious about his lack of success so far. But he was determined to get what was rightfully his. His face was contorted with jealous rage as the sister's house faded from view. As he drove back to his camper, he steeled himself for whatever battles lie ahead with the sisters. Tomorrow was another day and he still needed answers before plotting his next move.

"Turn the page for the glossary and the Sister's special Manhattan recipe."

Glossary

Denney: Well, I never!

Kat: Never what, as if that were possible?

Denney: That was Beau Buford on the phone just now.

Kat: Really…?

Denney: He said he and his missus had been taking some classes and he thought of me when the lecture was on communication.

Kat: And…?

Denney: He said he had confirmation that people like me shouldn't use words with which others might not be familiar. I told him to name some. Then he said, **dipsomaniac**.

Kat: Was he talking about us? Was he saying we were drunkards?

Denney: Don't know. Next, he got all arrogant and asked me, "what about **Narthex?**"

Kat: Then he ought to talk to Mildred Purvis. She would set him straight about it being the entryway to the church before the sanctuary.

Denney: Of course. Then he said, "okay, what about **espalier?**" Can you believe anyone in New Orleans doesn't know that one?

Kat: Not that he has ever been to our home, but you couldn't miss that bower of climbing flowers. Everyone has one or maybe two.

Denney: Well, the last one he threw out was **squiffy**. He's been in enough bars to know when he's a little tight. Hell, he's squiffy most of the time.

Kat: Try not to let it upset you. If he learns only one thing about himself in those classes, he will be 100% improved. Pray for him.

About the Authors

Kathy Steele is a sister, retired registered nurse, and part-time pre-school teacher. She is an avid reader.

Linda George is a sister, retired attorney, professor, and part-time mediator. She reads mostly boring stuff.

KAT AND DENNEY'S
SECRET MANHATTAN RECIPE

We are trusting, dear Reader, that you will keep this personal recipe close to your chest, so to speak. If you withhold the recipe, it's guaranteed to taste better. If you are asked to share the recipe, tell the requester that Amazon has it (Kindle, $3.99 and Paperback $14.95.) *And please, please drink responsibly.* You are not a fiction.

- 1 oz. Maker's Mark Bourbon
- 1 oz. Martini and Rossi Sweet Vermouth
- 3 Amarena Fabbri wild cherries
- 1 scant teaspoon of the cherry syrup

Serve over three ice cubes in your best crystal rocks glasses, unless served neat. In that case, serve in your best martini stems.

Note: We only use one dash of Angostura bitters in the Fall when we feel woodsy, which is practically never. Make substitutions at your own risk.

Thank you!

Thank you for purchasing this book and reading it all the way through. My sister and I hope you enjoyed it. We appreciate all feedback and especially any reviews you graciously upload to your favorite online bookseller.

Coming soon!

The Kat and Denney Archives: Book 2

Bourbon, Bahamas, and Bad Guys

Ordering Information

Orange Horse Press
3735 Palomar Centre Dr.
Ste. 150 (#35)
Lexington KY 40513
https://www.katanddenneyarchives.com/

Bourbon & Benjamins

Bourbon & Benjamins

·

Made in the USA
Middletown, DE
11 June 2022

66919013R00132